PENGUIN BOOKS

DELHI IS NOT FAR

Ruskin Bond's first novel, *The Room on the Roof*, written when he was seventeen, received the John Llewellyn Rhys Memorial Prize in 1957. Since then he has written a number of novellas, essays, poems and children's books, many of which have been published by Penguin. He has also written over 500 short stories and articles that have appeared in magazines and anthologies. He received the Sahitya Akademi Award in 1992, the Padma Shri in 1999 and the Padma Bhushan in 2014.

Ruskin Bond was born in Kasauli, Himachal Pradesh, and grew up in Jamnagar, Dehradun, New Delhi and Shimla. As a young man, he spent four years in the Channel Islands and London. He returned to India in 1955. He now lives in Landour, Mussoorie, with his adopted family.

Delhi is not far

RUSKIN BOND

PENGUIN BOOKS

An imprint of Penguin Random House

PENGUIN BOOKS

USA | Canada | UK | Ireland | Australia
New Zealand | India | South Africa | China

Penguin Books is part of the Penguin Random House group of companies
whose addresses can be found at global.penguinrandomhouse.com

Published by Penguin Random House India Pvt. Ltd
7th Floor, Infinity Tower C, DLF Cyber City,
Gurgaon 122 002, Haryana, India

Penguin
Random House
India

First published in Viking by Penguin Books India 2003
Published in Penguin Books 2005

Copyright © Ruskin Bond 1994, 2003

An abridged version of this novella first appeared in *Delhi Is Not Far: The Best of Ruskin Bond*, published by Penguin Books India in 1994.

All rights reserved

10 9 8

ISBN 9780143440437

Typeset in New Baskerville by S.R. Enterprises, New Delhi
Printed at Replika Press Pvt. Ltd, India

www.penguin.co.in

MIX
Paper from
responsible sources
FSC
www.fsc.org   FSC® C016779

For Ravi Singh,
who had faith in this
little-known story of mine

'Oh yes, I have known love, and again love,
   and many other kinds of love;
   but of that tenderness I felt then,
      is there nothing I can say?'
                    —Andre Gide, *Fruits of the Earth*

'If I am not for myself, who will be for me?
   And if I am not for others, what am I?
      And if not now, when?
                    —Hillel (Ancient Hebrew Sage)

Introduction

I wrote this novella back in the 1960s, when I left Dehra Dun for New Delhi. I thought I would find fame and fortune in the capital; I found nothing of the sort. And so, in the mid-1960s, I made for the hills, where I did at least find space and contentment. Over the years, this story was revised to a certain extent and was even at one time cut down to short-story length. Most of the original material was restored when Penguin India published it in the collection *Delhi Is Not Far: The Best of Ruskin Bond* in 1994: the only time it appeared between book covers. Now, slightly revised, it appears in this new edition.

Is this rather plotless tale of any relevance today? I think so, because there are many small towns like Pipalnagar that still exist, almost unchanged; and the preoccupations of their inhabitants haven't changed either. Making a living, looking for a better life, and believing that love and friendship are forever.

All over northern India, and in many other parts of the country, there are small towns, large towns, overgrown villages, where frustrated young men and women dream of a better life, whether it be in our cities or in a foreign land. Few escape into the bigger world, and those who do may not always find what they are looking for. The opportunities are limited, even in 'high-tech' India. We hear a lot about the information technology boom, but this has yet to filter down to small-town India, where thousands of youngsters pour out of schools and colleges with nowhere to go and nothing to do. Sometimes it's better to be a barber like Deep Chand or a rickshaw-puller like Pitamber than a degree-holder without a job. Last year, at a local college, there were nearly a thousand high school lads applying for one job of a chaprasi. I asked one disappointed candidate what he was going to do. 'Open a tea shop,' he said. Now most towns like Pipalnagar have hundreds of tea shops.

For a struggling freelance writer like Arun, there are more opportunities today. Writing scripts for TV serials is probably less soul-destroying than devising answer papers and writing crude thrillers. But for the publishing boom of the 1990s, many of my own stories, including this one, would have remained in limbo or been buried in the files of newspapers.

You won't find Pipalnagar on the map. It's an amalgam of small towns I had seen or lived in—Roorkee, Shamli, Meerut,

Saharanpur, Chhutmalpur . . . the list is endless. They have grown bigger, more congested; but they are still unsophisticated places, uninviting and unromantic on first acquaintance. But romance lurks in the most unlikely places. My Suraj, my Kamla, are still there, striving to break out of their little cages.

How evanescent those loves and friendships seem at this distance in time. I wonder what they are doing now, the people on whom these characters are modelled, if indeed they have survived. We move on, make new attachments. We grow old. But sometimes we hanker for the old friendships, the old loves. Sometimes I wish I was young again. Or that I could travel back in time and pick up the threads. Absent so long, I may have stopped loving you, friends; but I will never stop loving the days I loved you.

Ruskin Bond
January 2003

My balcony is my window on the world. I prefer it to my room.

The room has just one window, a square hole in the wall crossed by three iron bars. The view from it is a restricted one. If I crane my neck sideways, and put my nose to the bars, I can see the extremities of the building. If I stand on tiptoe and lean forward, I can see part of the narrow courtyard below where children—the children of all classes of people—play together. (When they are older, they will become conscious of the barriers of class and caste.)

Across the courtyard, on a level with my room, are three separate windows, belonging to three separate rooms, each window barred in the same unimaginative way. During the day it is difficult to look into these rooms. The harsh, cruel sunlight fills the courtyard, making the windows patches of darkness.

My room is small. I have paced about in it so often that I know its exact measurements. My foot, from heel to toe, is eleven inches. That makes the room just over twelve feet in length; when I measure the last foot, my toes turn up against the wall. In breadth, the room is exactly seven feet.

The plaster has been peeling off the walls, and there are many greasy stains and patches which are difficult to hide. I cover the worst stains with pictures cut from magazines, but as there is no symmetry about the stains there is none about the pictures. My personal effects are few, and none of them precious.

On a shelf in the wall are a pile of paperbacks, in English, Hindi and Urdu; among them my two Urdu thrillers, *Khoon* (Blood) and *Jasoos* (Detective). They did not take long to write. Some passages were my own, some free translations from English authors. Having been brought up in a Hindu home in a Muslim city—and in an English school—I was fairly proficient in three languages. The books have sold quite well—for my publisher . . .

My publisher, who operates from a Meerut by-lane, paid me two hundred rupees for each book; a flat and final payment, no royalties. I could not get better terms from any other publisher. It is a good country for publishers but not for writers. To quote Byron: 'Now Barabbas was a publisher . . .'

'If you want to make money, Arun,' he confided in me when he handed me my last cheque, 'publish your own books. Not detective stories. They have a limited market. Haven't you realized that India is fuller than ever of young people trying to pass exams? It is a desperate matter, this race for academic qualifications. Half the entrants fall by the wayside. The other half are even more unfortunate. They pass their exams and then they fall by the wayside. The point is, millions are sitting for exams, for MA, BSc, Ph.D . . . They all want to get these degrees the easy way, without reading too many books or attending more than half a dozen lectures— and that's where a smart person like you comes in! Why should they wade through five volumes of political history when they can get a dozen model answer papers? They are seldom wrong, the guess papers. All you have to do is make friends with someone on the University Board, write your papers, print them cheaply—never mind a few printing errors—and flood the market. They'll sell like hot cakes,' he concluded, using an English expression.

I told him I would think about his proposal, but I never really liked the idea. I preferred spilling the blood of fictitious prostitutes to spoon-feeding the brains of misguided students.

Besides, it would have been very boring.

A friend who shall be nameless offered to teach me the art of pickpocketing. But I had to give up after a few clumsy attempts on his pocket. To pick someone's pocket successfully is an art. My friend practised his craft at various railway stations and made a good living from it. I knew I could not. I would have to stick to writing cheap thrillers.

2

The string of my charpai needs tightening. The dip in the middle of the bed is so pronounced that invariably I wake up in the morning with a backache. But I am hopeless at tightening charpai strings and will have to wait until one of the boys from the tea-shop pays me a visit.

Under the charpai is my tin trunk. Its contents range from old, rejected manuscripts to photographs, clothes, newspaper cuttings and all that goes with the floating existence of an itinerant bachelor.

I do not live entirely alone. Sometimes a beggar, if he is not diseased, spends the night on the balcony; during cold or rainy weather the boys from the tea-shop, who normally sleep on the pavement, crowd into my room. But apart from them, there are the lizards on the walls—friends, these—

and a large rat who gets in and out of the window and carries away manuscripts and clothing; definitely an enemy.

*

June nights are the most uncomfortable of all. Mosquitoes emerge from all the ditches and gullies and ponds, and take over control of Pipalnagar. Bugs, finding it uncomfortable inside the woodwork of the charpai, scramble out at night and find their way under my sheet. I wrap myself up in the sheet like a corpse, but the mosquitoes bite through the thin material, and the bugs get in at the tears and holes.

The lizards wander listlessly over the walls, impatient for the monsoon rains, when they will be able to feast off thousands of insects.

Everyone is waiting for the cool, quenching relief of the monsoon. But two months from now, when roofs have fallen in, the road is flooded, and the drinking water contaminated, we will be cursing the monsoon and praying for its speedy retreat.

To wake in the morning in summer is not difficult, as sleep is fitful, uneasy, crowded with dreams and fantasies. I know it is five o'clock when I hear the first bus coming out of the shed. If I am to defecate in private, I must be up and away into the fields beyond the railway tracks. The public lavatory near the station hasn't been cleaned for over a week.

Afterwards I return to the balcony and, slipping out of my vest and pyjamas, rub down my body with mustard oil. If the boy from the tea-shop is awake, I get him to massage me, while I lie flat on my back or on my belly, dreaming of things less mundane than life in Pipalnagar.

I dream of Delhi, only two hundred miles away, where so much is happening: Five Year Plans (so the papers say), and plans for big dams, airports, new industries, and a grand new city coming up in Chandigarh. I see all this in the newsreels at our local cinema, along with pictures of a smiling Mr Nehru laying foundation stones for his 'new temples of India'. And pictures of him playing with his grandchildren, waving to adoring crowds, or walking in his rose garden. Oh, for a rose garden in Pipalnagar. It might inspire me to write my own *Gulistan*!

*

As the passengers alight from the first bus of the day into Pipalnagar, I sit in the barber shop and talk to Deep Chand while he lathers my face with soap. The knife moves cleanly across my cheeks and throat, and Deep Chand's breath, smelling of cloves and cardamoms—he is a perpetual eater of paan—plays on my face. In the next chair the sweetmeat-seller is having the hair shaved from under his great flabby armpits; he is looked after by Deep Chand's younger brother,

Ramu, who is deputed to attend to the less popular customers. Ramu flashes a smile at me when I enter the shop; we have had a couple of nocturnal excursions together.

Deep Chand is a short, thick-set man, very compact, dark and smooth-skinned from his waist upwards. Below his waist, from his hips to his ankles, he is a mass of soft black hair. An extremely virile man, he is very attractive to women.

Deep Chand and Ramu know all there is to know about me—in fact, all there is to know about Pipalnagar.

'When are you going to get married, brother?' Deep Chand asked me recently.

'Oh, after five or ten years,' I replied.

'You are twenty-five now,' he said. 'This is the time to marry. Once you are thirty, it will not be so easy to find a wife. In Pipalnagar, when you are thirty you are old.'

'I feel too old already,' I said. 'Don't talk to me of marriage, but give a massage. My brain is not functioning well these days. In my latest book I have killed three people in one chapter, and still it is dull.'

'Well, finish it soon,' said Deep Chand, beginning the ritual of the head-massage. 'Then you can clear your debts. When you have paid your debts you will leave Pipalnagar, won't you?'

I could not answer because he had started thumping my skull with his hard, communicative fingers, tugging at the roots of my hair, and squeezing my temples with the palms of his hands. No one gave a better massage than Deep Chand. Had his income been greater, he could have shifted his trade to another locality and made a decent living. Here, in our Mohalla, his principal customers were shopkeepers, truck drivers, labourers from the railway station. He charged only two rupees for a hair-cut; in other places it was three rupees.

While Deep Chand ran his fingers through my hair, exerting a gentle pressure on my temples, I made a mental inventory of all the people who owed me money and to whom I was in debt.

The amounts I had loaned out—to various bazaar acquaintances—were small compared to the amounts I owed others. There was my landlord, Seth Govind Ram, who was in fact the landlord of half Pipalnagar and the proprietor of the dancing-girls—they did everything but dance—who lived in a dormitory near the bus stop; I owed him six months' rent. Sixty rupees.

He does not bother me just now, but in six months' time he will be after my blood, and I will have to pay up somehow.

Seth Govind Ram possesses a bank, a paunch and, allegedly, a mistress. The bank and the paunch are both conspicuous landmarks in Pipalnagar. Few people have seen his mistress. She is kept hidden away in an enormous Rajput-style house outside the city, and continues to be a challenge to my imagination.

Seth Govind Ram is a prominent member of the municipality. Publicly, he is a staunch supporter of the ruling party; privately, he supports all parties with occasional contributions towards their funds. He owns, as I have said, most of the buildings in the Pipalnagar Mohalla; and though he is always promising to pull them down and build new ones, he finds it more profitable to leave them as they are.

Perhaps some day I really will settle my debts with Seth Govind Ram. Aziz believes that I will. Aziz visits me occasionally for a loan of two or three rupees, which he returns in kind, whenever I visit his junk shop. He is a Muslim boy of eighteen. He lives in a small room behind the junk shop.

The shop has mud walls and a tin roof. The walls are always in danger of being washed away during the monsoon, and the roof of sailing away during a dust-storm. The rain comes in, anyway, and the floor is awash most of the time; bound copies of old English magazines gather mildew, and the pots and pans and spare parts grow rusty. Aziz, at eighteen, is beginning to collect dust and age and disease.

But he is an optimistic soul, even though there is nothing for him to be optimistic about, and he is always asking me when I intend keeping my vow of going to Delhi to make my fortune. He does not doubt that I will. I am to keep an eye out for a favourable shop-site near Chandni Chowk where he can open a more up-to-date junk shop. He is saving towards this end; but what he saves trickles away in paying for his wife's upkeep at the Pipalnagar Home, where he was forced to send her after his family pronounced her insane. Pipalnagar has many candidates for the Home, but it's a place of last resort; no one ever comes back.

3

My efforts at making a fortune were many and varied. I had, for three days, kept a vegetable stall; invested in an imaginary tea-shop; and even tried my hand as a palmist. This last venture was a failure, not because I was a poor palmist—I had intuition enough to be able to guess what a man or woman would be happy to know—but because prospective customers were few in Pipalnagar. My friends and neighbours had grown far too cynical of the future to expect any bonuses.

'When a child is born,' asserted Deep Chand, 'his fists are clenched. They have been clenched for so long that little creases form on his palms. That is the only meaning in our lines. What have they to do with our future?'

I agreed with Deep Chand, but I thought fortune-telling might be an easy way of making money. Others did it, from saffron-robed sadhus to BAs and BComs, and did it fairly successfully, so that I felt I should try it too. It did not take me long to read a book on the subject, and to hang a board from my balcony, announcing my profession. That I did not succeed was probably due to the fact that I was too well-known in Pipalnagar. Half the Mohalla thought it was a joke; the other half, quite understandably, didn't believe in my genuineness.

The vegetable stall was more exciting. Down the road, near the clock tower, a widow kept a grocery store. She sold rice, spices, pulses, almost everything except meat and vegetables. The widow did not think vegetables were worth the risk of an initial investment, but she was determined to try them out, and persuaded me to put up the money.

I found it difficult to refuse. She was a strong woman, ample-bosomed, known to fight in public with any man who tried to get the better of her. She was a persuasive saleswoman, too, and soon had me conjuring up visions of a vegetable stall of my own full of succulent fruits and fresh green vegetables.

Full it was, from beginning to end. I didn't sell a single cabbage or cauliflower or salad leaf. Before the vegetables went bad, I gave them away to Deep Chand, Pitamber, and other friends. The widow had insisted that I charge ten paise per kilo more than others charged, a disastrous thing to do in Pipalnagar, where the question of preferring quality to quantity did not arise. She said that for the extra ten paise customers would get cleaner and greener vegetables. She was wrong. Customers wanted them cleaner and greener and cheaper.

Still, it had been exciting on the first morning, getting up at five (I hadn't done this for years) and walking down to the vegetable market near the railway station, haggling with the wholesalers, piling the vegetables into baskets, and leading the coolie back to the bazaar with a proprietorial air.

The railway station, half a mile from the bus stop, had always attracted me. As a boy I had been fascinated by trains (as I suppose most boys are), and waved to the passengers as the trains flew through the fields, and was always delighted when one of them waved back to me. I had wondered about the people in the carriages—where they were going, and why... Trains had meant romance, escape into another world. Until the Nawabgunj crash that took my parents' lives. That set me adrift, but it was the end of romance.

'What you should do,' advised Deep Chand, while he lathered my face with soap—(there were several reasons why I did not shave myself; laziness, the desire to gossip, the fact that Deep Chand used his razor as an artist uses a brush . . .)— 'What you should do, is marry a wealthy woman. It would solve all your problems. She would be only too happy to possess a young man of sexual accomplishments. You could then do your writing at leisure, with slaves to fan you and press your legs.'

'Not a bad idea,' I said, 'but where does one find such a woman? I expect Seth Govind Ram has a wife in addition to a mistress, but I have never seen her; and the Seth doesn't look as though he is going to die.'

'She doesn't have to be a widow. Find a young woman who is married to a fat and important millionaire. She will support you.' Deep Chand was a married man himself, with several children. I had never bothered to count them.

His children, and others, give one the impression that in Pipalnagar children outnumber adults five to one. This is really the case, I suppose. The census tells us that one in four of our population is in the age-group of five to fifteen years. They swarm over the narrow streets, appearing to belong to one vast family—a race of pot-bellied little men, half-naked, dusty, quarrelling and laughing and crying and having so little in common with the race of adults who have brought them into the world.

On either side of my room there are families, each with about a dozen members—each family living in a room a little bigger than mine, which is used for cooking, eating, sleeping and loving. The men work in the sugar factory and bring home about fifty rupees a month. The older children attend the Pipalnagar High School, and come home only for their food. The younger ones are in and out all day, their pockets full of stones and marbles and small coins.

Tagore wrote: 'Every child comes with the message that God is not yet discouraged of man.'

At noon, when the shadows shift and cross the road, a band of children rush down the empty, silent street, shouting and waving their satchels. They have been at their desks from early morning, and now, despite the hot sun, they will have their fling while their elders sleep on string charpais beneath leafy neem trees.

On the soft sand near the river-bed boys wrestle or play leapfrog. At alley-corners, where tall buildings shade narrow passages, the favourite game is gulli-danda. Elsewhere, in open spaces, it is kabaddi, a game for both children and young men. It is a village game, and calls for good control of the breath and much agility and strength.

Pitamber, a young wrestler who migrated here from a nearby village only recently, excels at kabbadi. He knows all the holds, and is particularly adept at capturing an opponent. He took me to his village once. All the boys there were long-limbed and sun-browned, erect and at the same time relaxed. There is a sense of vitality and confidence in Pitamber's village, which I have not seen in Pipalnagar.

In Pipalnagar there is not exactly despair, but resignation, an indifference to both living and dying. The town is almost truly reflected in the Pipalnagar Home, where in an open courtyard surrounded by mud walls a score of mental patients wander about, listless and bored. A man jabbers excitedly, but most of the inmates are quiet, sad and resentful.

Such sights depress me sometimes. The world seems crowded with unfinished lives.

'I wonder why God ever bothered to make men, when he had the whole wide beautiful world to himself,' I said to Suraj one summer night. 'Why did he find it necessary to share it with others?'

'Perhaps he felt lonely,' said Suraj.

4

I do not know if Suraj ever wished that our first meeting had been different. He never talked about it.

I was walking through the fields beyond the railway tracks, when I saw someone lying on the footpath, his head and body hidden by the ripening wheat. The wheat was shaking where he lay, and as I came nearer I saw that one of his legs kept twitching convulsively.

Thinking that perhaps it was a case of robbery with violence, I prepared to run; but then, cursing myself for being a shallow coward, I approached the agitated person.

He was a youth of about eighteen, and he appeared to be in the throes of a violent fit.

His face was white, except where a little blood had trickled from his mouth. His leg kept twitching, and his hands moved restlessly, helplessly amongst the wheat.

I spoke to him: 'What is wrong?' I asked, but he was obviously unconscious and could not answer. So I ran down the path to the well, and dipping the end of my shirt in a shallow trough of water, soaked it well, and ran back to the boy.

By that time he seemed to have recovered from the fit. The twitching had ceased, and though he still breathed heavily, his face was calm and his hands still. I wiped the blood from his mouth, and he opened his eyes and stared at me without any immediate comprehension.

'You have bitten your tongue.' I said. 'There's no hurry. I'll stay here with you.'

We rested where we were for some minutes without saying anything. He was no longer agitated. Resting his chin on his knees, he passed his hands around his drawn-up legs.

'I am all right now,' he said.

'What happened?'

'It was nothing, it often happens. I don't know why. I cannot stop it.'

'Have you seen a doctor?'

'I went to the hospital when it first began. They gave me some pills. I had to take them every day. But they made me so tired and sleepy that I couldn't do any work. So I stopped taking them. I get the attack about once a week, but I am useless if I take those pills.'

He got to his feet, smiling as he dusted his clothes.

He was a thin boy, long-limbed and bony. There was a little fluff on his cheeks and the promise of a moustache. His pyjamas were short for him, accentuating the awkwardness of his long, bony feet. He had beauty, though; his eyes held secrets, his mouth hesitant smiles.

He told me that he was a student at the Pipalnagar College, and that his terminal examination would be held in August. Apparently his whole life hinged on the result of the coming examination. If he passed, there was the prospect of a scholarship, and eventually a place for himself in the world. If he failed, there was only the prospect of Pipalnagar, and a living eked out by selling combs and buttons and little vials of perfume.

I noticed the tray of merchandise lying on the ground. It usually hung at his waist, the straps going round his neck. All day he walked about Pipalnagar, covering ten to fifteen miles a day, selling odds and ends to people at their houses. He made about two rupees a day, which gave him enough for his food; and he ate irregularly, at little tea-shops, at the stalls near the bus stops, or on the roadside under shady jamun and mango trees. When the jamuns were ripe, he would sit in a tree, sucking the sour fruit till his lips were stained purple with their juice. There was always the fear that he would get a fit while sitting in a tree, and fall off; but the temptation to eat jamuns was too great for him, and he took the risk.

'Where do you stay?' I asked. 'I will walk back with you to your home.'

'I don't stay anywhere in particular. Sometimes in a dharamsala, sometimes in the Gurudwara, sometimes on the Maidan. In the summer months I like to sleep on the Maidan, on the grass.'

'Then I'll walk with you to the Maidan,' I said.

There was nothing extraordinary about his being a refugee and an orphan. During the communal holocaust of 1947 thousands of homes had been destroyed, women and children killed. What was extraordinary was his sensitivity—or should I say sensibility—a rare quality in a Punjabi youth who had been brought up in the Frontier Provinces during one of the most cruel periods in the country's history. It was not his conversation that impressed me—though his attitude to life was one of hope, while in Pipalnagar people were too resigned even to be desperate—but the gentle persuasiveness of his voice, eyes, and also of his hands, long-fingered, gliding hands, and his smile which flickered with amusement and sometimes irony.

5

One morning, when I opened the door of my room, I found Suraj asleep at the top of the steps. His tray lay a short distance away. I shook him gently, and he woke up immediately, blinking in the bright sunlight.

'Why didn't you come in,' I said. 'Why didn't you tell me?'

'It was late,' he said. 'I didn't want to disturb you.'

'Someone could have stolen your things while you slept.'

'So far no one has stolen from me.'

I made him promise to sleep in my room that night, and he came in at ten, curled up on the floor and slept fitfully, while I lay awake worrying if he was comfortable enough.

He came several nights, and left early in the morning, before I could offer him anything to eat. We would talk into the early hours of the morning. Neither of us slept much.

I liked Suraj's company. He dispelled some of my own loneliness, and I found myself looking forward to the sound of his footsteps on the stairs. He liked my company because I was full of stories, even though some of them were salacious; and because I encouraged his ambitions and gave him confidence.

I forget what it was I said that offended him and hurt his feelings—something unintentional, and, of course, silly: one of those things that you cannot remember afterwards but which seem terribly important at the time. I had probably been giving him too much advice, showing off my knowledge of the world and women, and joking about his becoming a prime minister one day: because the next night he didn't come to my room.

I waited till eleven o'clock for the sound of his footsteps, and then when he didn't come, I left the room and went in search of him. I couldn't bear the thought of an angry and unhappy Suraj sleeping alone on the Maidan. What if he should have another fit? I told myself that he had been through scores of fits without my being around to help him, but already I was beginning to feel protective towards him.

The shops had closed and lights showed only in upper windows. There were many sleeping on the sidewalk, and I peered into the faces of each, but I did not find Suraj. Eventually I found him on the Maidan, asleep on a bench.

'Suraj,' I said, and he awoke and sat up.

'What is it?'

'I've been looking for you for the last two hours. Come on home.'

'Why don't you spend the night here?' he said. 'This is my home.'

I felt angry at first, but then I felt ashamed of my anger.

I said, 'Thank you for your kind offer, my friend, it will be a privilege to be your guest,' and sat down on the bench beside him.

We were silent for some time, while a big yellow moon played hide and seek with the clouds. Then it began to drizzle.

'It's raining,' I said. 'Why didn't you make a roof over your house? Now let us go back to mine.'

I thought he might still refuse to return with me, but he got up, smiling; perhaps it was my own sudden humility, or perhaps it was the rain . . . I think it was my own humility, because it made him feel he had wronged me. He did not feel for himself that way, and so it was not the rain.

*

In the afternoon Pipalnagar is empty. The temperature has touched 106°F! To walk barefoot on the scorching pavement is possible only for the beggars and labourers whose feet have developed several layers of hard protective skin. And even they lie stretched out in the shade given by shops and walls, their open sores festering in the hot sun.

Suraj will be asleep in the shade of a peepul or banyan tree, a book lying open beside him, his tray a few feet away. Sometimes the crows are fascinated by his many coloured combs, and come down from the trees to inspect them.

At this hour of the day I lie naked on the stone floor of my room, because the floor is the coolest place of all; and as I am too listless to work or sleep, I study my navel, the hair on my belly, the languid aspect of my genitals, and the hair on my legs and thighs. I study my toes, and with the dust that has accumulated on my feet, I trace patterns on the walls and disturb the flaking plaster which in itself has formed a score of patterns—birds and snakes and elephants . . . With a little imagination I can conjure up the entire world of the *Panchatantra* . . .

Of all the joys of the senses, I think it is the sense of touch I relish most—contact of the cool floor on a hot day. That is why I lie naked in my room, so that all my flesh is in touch with the cool stones.

The touch of the earth—soft earth, stony earth, grass, mud. Sometimes the road is so hot that it scorches the most hardened feet; sometimes it is cold and hard and cruel. Grass is good, especially dew-drenched grass; then the feet are stained with juices, and the sap seems to pass into the body. Wet earth is soft and sensuous, and when the mud cakes on one's feet it is interesting to bathe at a tap and watch the muddy water run away, like a young stream eager to reach elsewhere.

*

There are days and there are nights, and then there are other days and other nights, and all the days and nights in Pipalnagar are the same.

A few things reassure me . . . The desire to love and be loved. The beauty and ugliness of the human body, the intricacy of its design. Sometimes I make love as a sort of exploration of all that is physical; and sometimes falling in love becomes an exploration of the mind. Love takes me to distant, happier places.

6

It is difficult to fall asleep some nights. Apart from the mosquitoes and the oppressive atmosphere, there are the loudspeakers blaring all over Pipalnagar—at cinemas, marriages and religious gatherings. There is a continuous variety of fare—religious music and film music. I do not care much for either, and yet I am compelled to listen, both repelled and fascinated by the sounds that permeate the midnight air.

Strangely enough, it does not trouble Suraj. He is immune to noise. Once he is asleep, it would take a bomb to disturb him. At the first blare of the loudspeaker, he pulls a pillow or towel over his head, and falls asleep. He has been in Pipalnagar longer than I, and has grown accustomed to living against a background of noise. And yet he is a silent person, silent in his movements and in his moods; and I, who love silence so much—I am clumsy and garrulous.

Suraj does not know if his parents are dead or alive. He lost them, literally, when he was seven.

His father had been a cultivator, a dark unfathomable man, who spoke little, thought perhaps even less, and was vaguely aware that he possessed a son—a weak boy, who resembled his mother to a disconcerting degree in that he not only looked like her but was given to introspection and dawdling at the river-bank when he should have been at work in the fields.

The boy's mother was a subdued, silent woman—frail and consumptive. Her husband did not expect that she would live long. Perhaps the separation from her son put an end to her interest in life—or perhaps it has urged her to live on somewhere, in the hope that she will find him again.

Suraj lost his parents at Amritsar railway station, where trains coming over the border disgorged themselves of thousands of refugees—or pulled into the station half-empty, drenched with blood and piled with corpses.

Suraj and his parents were lucky to escape the massacre. Had they been able to travel on an earlier train (they had tried desperately to get into one) they might easily have been killed; but circumstances favoured them then, only to trick them later.

Suraj was clinging to his mother's sari, while she kept close to her husband, who was elbowing his way through the frightened, bewildered throng of refugees. Looking over his shoulder at a woman sobbing on the ground, Suraj collided with a burly Sikh and lost his grip on his mother's sari.

The Sikh had a long, curved sword at his waist, and Suraj stared up at him in terror and fascination, at his long hair, which had fallen loose, and his wild black beard, and the blood-stains on his white shirt. The Sikh pushed him out of the way, and when Suraj looked round for his mother she was not to be seen.

He could hear her calling to him, 'Suraj, where are you, Suraj?' and he tried to force his way through the crowd, in the direction of her voice, but he was carried the other way.

7

At a certain age a boy is like young wheat, growing, healthy, on the verge of manhood. His eyes are alive, his mind quick, his gestures confident. You cannot mistake him.

This is the most fascinating age, when a boy becomes a man—it is interesting both physically and mentally: the growth of the boy's hair, the toning of the muscles, the consciousness of growing and changing and maturing—never again will there be so much change and development in so short a period of time. The body exudes virility, is full of currents and counter-currents.

For a girl, puberty is a frightening age when alarming things begin to happen to her body; for a boy it is an age of self-assertion, of a growing confidence in himself and in his attitude to the world. His physical changes are a source of happiness and pride.

In Suraj, I see all of this. I do not envy him; I am happy for him, and with him.

*

There were no inhibitions in my friendship with Suraj. We spoke of bodies as we spoke of minds, and discussed the problems of one as we would discuss those of the other, for they are really the same problems.

He was beautiful, with the beauty of the short-lived, a transient, sad beauty. It made me sad sometimes even to look at his pale slim limbs. It hurt me to look into his eyes. There was death in his eyes.

He told me that he was afraid of women, that he constantly felt the urge to possess a woman, but that when confronted with one he might just as well have been a eunuch.

I told him that not every woman was made for every man, and that I would bring him a girl with whom he would be happy.

This was Kamla, a very friendly person from the house run by Seth Govind Ram. She was very small, and rather delicate, but more skilled in love-making than any of her colleagues. She was patient, and particularly fond of the young and inexperienced. She was only twenty-three, but had been four years in the profession.

*

Kamla's hands and feet are beautiful. That in itself is satisfying. A beautiful face leaves me cold if the hands and feet are ugly. Perhaps this is some sort of phobia with me.

Kamla first met me when I came up the stairs shortly after I had moved into the room above the bus stop. She was sitting on the steps, eating a melon; and when she saw me, she smiled and held out a slice.

'Will you eat melon, bhai sahib?' she asked, and her voice was so appealing and her eyes so mischievous that I couldn't help taking the melon from her hands.

'Sit down,' she said, patting the step. I had never come across a girl so openly friendly and direct. As I sat down, I discovered the secret of her smile; it lay in the little scar on her right check; when she smiled, the scar turned into a dimple.

'Don't you do any work?' she asked.

'I write stories and things,' I said.

'Is that work?'

'Well, I live by it.'

'Show me,' she demanded.

I brought her a magazine and began turning the pages for her. She could read a little, if the words were simple enough. But she didn't get as far as my story, because her attention was arrested by a picture of a girl with an urchin hair-cut.

'It is a girl?' she asked; and, when I assured her it was: 'But her hair, how is it like that?'

'That's the latest fashion,' I protested. 'Thousands of women keep hair like that. At least they did a year ago,' I added, looking at the date on the magazine.

'Is it easy to make?'

'Yes, you just take a pair of scissors and cut away until it looks untidy enough.'

'I like it. You give it to me. I'll go and get scissors.'

'No, no!' I said. 'You can't do that, your family will be most upset.'

She stamped her bare foot on the step. 'I have no family, silly man! I have a husband who is happy only if I can make myself attractive to others. He is skinny and smells of garlic, and he has given my father five acres of land for the favour of having a wife half his age. But it is Seth Govind Ram who really owns me; my husband is only his servant.'

'Why are you telling me all this?'

'Why shouldn't I tell you?' she said, and gave me a dark, defiant look. 'You like me, do you not?'

'Of course I like you,' I hastened to assure her.

*

I think I hate families. I am jealous of them. Their sense of security, of interdependence, infuriates me. To every family I am an outsider, because I have no family. A man without a family is a social outcast. He has no credentials. A man's credentials are his father and his father's property. His mother is another quantity; it is her family—her father—that matter.

So I am glad that I do not belong to a family, and at the same time sad, because in our country if you do not belong to a family you are a piece of driftwood. And so two pieces of driftwood come together, and finding themselves caught in the same current, move along with it until they are trapped in a counter-current, and dispersed.

And that is the way it is with me. I must cling to someone as long as circumstances will permit it.

*

Having no family of our own, it was odd and even touching that Kamla should have adopted us both as her brothers during the Raksha Bandhan festival.

It was a change to have Kamla visiting us early in the morning instead of late at night; and we were surprised, and rather disconcerted, to be treated as her brothers.

She tied the silver tinsel round our wrists, and I said, 'Kamla, we are proud to be your brothers, and we would like to make you some gift, but at the moment there is no money with us.'

'I want your protection, not your money,' said Kamla. 'I want to feel that I am not alone in the world.'

So that made three of us. But we could hardly call ourselves a family.

*

Kamla visited us about once a week, when she found time to spare from her professional duties.

I think she preferred Suraj to me. He was gentle and he was beautiful, and I think she felt, as I did, that he would not live very long. She wanted to give him as much of herself as she could in so short a time.

Suraj was always a bit embarrassed with her around. At first I thought it was because of my presence in the room; but when I offered to leave, he protested. He told me that he would have been completely helpless if I was not present all the time.

Suraj and I were sitting in the tea-shop one night. Most of the customers were outside on a bench, where they could listen to the shopkeeper, a popular story-teller. Sitting on the ground in front of the shop was a thick-set youth, with a shaved head. He was dumb—they called him Goonga—and the customers often made sport of him, abusing him and clouting him over the head from time to time. The Goonga didn't mind this; he made faces at the others, and chuckled derisively at their remarks. He could say only one word, 'Goo,' and he said it often. This kept the customers in fits of laughter.

'Goo,' he said, when he saw Suraj enter the shop with me. He pointed at us, chuckled, and said, 'Goo.'

Everyone laughed. Someone got up from the bench and, with the flat of his hand, whacked the Goonga over his bald head. The Goonga sprang at the man making queer noises in his throat, and then someone tripped him and sent him sprawling on the ground. There was more laughter.

We were sitting at an inside table, and everyone was drinking tea, except the Goonga.

'Give the Goonga a glass of tea,' I told the shopkeeper. The shopkeeper grinned but complied with the order. The Goonga looked at me and said, 'Goo.'

When we left the shop, the full moon floated above us, robbing the stars of their glory. We walked in the direction of the Maidan, towards my room. The bazaar was almost empty, the shops closed. I became conscious of the sound of soft footfalls behind me and, looking over my shoulder, found that we were being followed by the Goonga.

'Goo,' he said, on being noticed.

'Why did you have to give him tea?' said Suraj. 'Now he probably thinks we are rich, and won't let us out of sight again.'

'He can do no harm,' I said, though I quickened my step. 'We'll pretend we're going to sleep on the Maidan, then he'll change his mind about us.'

'Goo,' said the Goonga from behind, and quickened his step as well.

We turned abruptly down an alley-way, trying to shake him off; but he padded after us, chuckling ghoulishly to himself. We cut back to the main road, but he was behind us at the clock tower. At the edge of the Maidan I turned and said:

'Go away, Goonga. We've got very little, and can't do anything for you. Go away.'

But the youth said 'Goo' and took a step forward, and his shaved head glistened in the moonlight. I shrugged, and led Suraj on to the Maidan. The Goonga stood at the edge of the Maidan, shaking his head and chuckling to himself. His body showed through his rags, and his feet were covered with mud. He watched us as we walked across the grass, watched us until we sat down on a bench; then he shrugged his shoulders and said 'Goo' and went away.

*

The beggars on the whole are a thriving community, and it came as no surprise to me when the municipality decided to place a tax on begging.

I know that some beggars earned, on an average, more than a chaprasi or a clerk; I knew for certain that the one-legged man, who had been hobbling about town on crutches long before I come to Pipalnagar, sent money orders home every month. Begging had become a profession, and so perhaps the municipality felt justified in taxing it, and besides, the municipal coffers needed replenishing.

Shaggy old Ganpat Ram, who was bent double and couldn't straighten up, didn't like it at all, and told me so. 'If I had known this was going to happen,' he mumbled, 'I would have chosen some other line of work.'

Ganpat Ram was an aristocrat among beggars. I had heard that he had once been a man of property, with several houses and a European wife; when his wife packed up and returned to Europe, together with all their savings, Ganpat had a nervous breakdown from which he never recovered. His health became steadily worse until he had to hobble about with a stick. He never made a direct request for money, but greeted you politely, commented on the weather or the price of things, and stood significantly beside you.

I suspected his story to be half true because whenever he approached a well-dressed person, he used impeccable English. He had a white beard and twinkling eyes, and was not the sort of beggar who invokes the names of the gods and calls on the mercy of the passer-by. Ganpat would rely more on a good joke. Some said he was a spy or a policeman in disguise, but so devoted to his work that he would probably remain a beggar for another five years.

I don't know how blind the blind man was, because he always recognized me in the street, even when he was alone. He would invoke blessings on my head, or curses, as the occasion demanded. I didn't like the blind man, because he made too much capital out of his affliction; there were opportunities for him to work with other blind people, but he found begging more profitable. The boy who sometimes led him around town didn't beg from me, but would ask, 'Have you got an anna on you?' as though he were merely borrowing the money, or needed it only for a minute or two. He was quite friendly, and even came up to my room, to see how I was getting on. He was very solicitous about my welfare. If he saw me from a hundred yards down the street, he would run all the way up to enquire about my health, and borrow an anna. He had a crafty, healthy face, and wore a long, dirty cloak draped over his shoulders, and very little else. He didn't care about the tax on begging, that was the blind man's problem.

In fact, the tax didn't affect the boys at all; with them, begging was a pastime and not a profession. They had big watery eyes, and it was difficult to resist their appeal.

'I haven't any small change,' I would say defensively.

'I'll change your note,' offers the boy.

'It's not a note; it's a fifty paise coin.'

'What do you want to change that for? Give me the coin and I won't trouble you for the rest of the week.'

'That's very kind of you.' But even if I gave him the two annas, he would accost me again at the first opportunity and wheedle something more from my pocket. There was a time when beggars asked for one or two pice; but these days, what with the rise in the cost of living, they never ask for anything less than an anna.

Friday is Leper Day. There is a leper colony a little way out of town, on the banks of a muddy, mosquito-ridden ditch, the other side of the railway station. The lepers come into Pipalnagar once a week to beg, and wander through the town in small groups, making for wealthy-looking individuals who give them something if only to avoid being followed down the road. (Of course the danger of contagion is very real, but if the municipal authorities do not let the lepers beg, they will have to support them, and that would prove expensive).

Some of the leper girls have good faces, but their hands are withered stumps, or their arms and legs are eaten away: the older ones have lost their ears and noses, and the men shuffle about with one or two limbs missing. Most of the sufferers belong to the hill areas, where it is still widely believed that leprosy is punishment for sins committed in a former life; the victim is ostracized and often driven out by his family; he goes into the towns and, in order to get work, makes a secret of his affliction; it is only when it can no longer be concealed that he goes for treatment, and then it is too late. The few who get into the hospitals are soldiers and policemen, who are looked after by the State, and a few others whose families have not disclaimed responsibility for them.

But the tax didn't affect the lepers either. It was aimed at the professionals, those who had made a business of begging over the past few years. It was rumoured that one beggar, after spending the day on the pavement calling for alms, would have a taxi drawn up beside him in the evening, and would be driven off to his residence outside town. And when, some months back, news got around that the Pipalnagar Bank was ready to crash, one beggar, who had never been seen to stand on his own two feet, leapt from the pavement and sprinted for the Bank. The professionals are usually crippled or maimed in one way or another—many of them have maimed themselves, others have gone through rigorous training schools in their youth, where they are versed in the fine art of begging. A few cases are genuine, and those are not so loud in their demands for charity, with the result that they don't make much. There are some who sing for their money, and I do not class these as beggars unless they sing badly.

Well, when the municipality decided to place a tax on begging, you should have seen the beggars get together; anyone would have thought they had a union. About a hundred of them took a procession down the main road to the municipal offices, shouting slogans and even waving banners to express the injustice felt by the beggar fraternity over this high-handed action of the authorities. They came on sticks and in carts, a dirty, ragged bunch, one or two of them stark naked; and they stood for two hours outside the municipal offices, to the embarrassment of the working staff and anyone who tried to enter the building.

Eventually somebody came out and told them it was all a rumour, and that no such tax had been contemplated; it would be far too impractical, for one thing. The beggars could all go home and hoard their earnings without any fear of official interference.

So the beggars returned jubilant, feeling they had won a moral victory, conscious of the power of group action. They went out of their way to develop their union, and now there is a fully fledged Beggars' Union. Different districts are allotted to different beggars, and woe betide the trespasser. It is even rumoured that they intend staging demonstrations outside the houses of those who refuse to be charitable!

But my own personal beggars, old Ganpat Ram and the boys, don't take advantage of their growing power; they treat me with due respect and affection; they do not consider me just another member of the public, who has to be blackmailed into charity, but look upon me as a friend who can be counted upon to make them a small loan from time to time, without expecting any immediate return.

9

'Should I go to Delhi, Suraj?'

'Why not? You are always talking about it. You should go.'

'I would like you to come with me. Perhaps they can make you better there, even cure you of your fits.'

'Not now. After my examinations.'

'Then I will wait . . .'

'Go now, if there is a chance of making a living in Delhi.'

'There is nothing definite. But I know the chance will not come until I leave this place and make my chances. There are one or two editors who have asked me to look them up. They could give me some work. And if I find an honest publisher I might be encouraged to write an honest book.'

'Write the book, even if you don't find a publisher.'

'I will try.'

We decided to save a little money, from his small earnings and from my occasional erratic payments which came by money order. I would need money for my trip to Delhi; sometimes there were medicines to be paid for; and we had no warm clothes for the cold weather. We managed to put away twenty rupees one week, but withdrew it the next, as Pitamber needed a loan for repairs on his cycle-rickshaw. He returned the money in three instalments and it disappeared in meeting various small bills.

Pitamber and Deep Chand and Ramu and Aziz all had plans for visiting Delhi. Only Kamla could not foresee such a move for herself. She was a woman and she had no man.

Deep Chand dreamt of his barber shop. Pitamber planned to own a scooter-rickshaw, which would involve no physical exertion and bring in more money. Ramu had a hundred-and-one different dreams, all of which featured beautiful women. He was a sweet boy, with little intelligence but much good nature.

Once, when he had his arm gashed by a knife in a street fight, he came to me for treatment. The hospital would have had to report the matter to the police. I washed his wound, poured benzedrine over it to stop the bleeding, and bandaged his arm rather crudely. He was very grateful and rewarded me with the story of his life. It was a chronicle of disappointed females, all of whom had been seduced by Ramu in fantastic circumstances and had been discarded by him after he had slept with each but once. Ramu boasted that he did not go twice to the same woman.

All this was good-natured lying, as it was well-known that a girl-teaser like Ramu had never seen anything more than a well-shaped ankle; but apparently Ramu believed in many of his own adventures, which in his own mind had acquired a legendary aspect.

I did not ask him how he got his arm cut, because I know he would have given me a fantastic explanation involving his honour and a lady's dishonour. Later I discovered that an irate brother had stabbed him for spreading discreditable rumours about his sister.

Ramu slept in my room that night. It was the sweet sleep of childhood. Suraj read his books, and Kamla came and went, while Ramu dreamt—he told us about it in the morning—of a woman with three breasts.

10

'Look, Ganpat,' I said one day, 'I've heard a lot of stories about you, and I don't know which is true. How did you get your crooked back?'

'That's a very long story,' he said, flattered by my interest in him. 'And I don't know if you will believe it. Besides, it is not to anyone that I would speak freely.'

He had served his purpose in whetting my appetite. I said, 'I'll give you four annas if you tell me your story. How about that?'

He stroked his beard, considering my offer. 'All right,' he said, squatting down on his haunches in the sunshine, while I pulled myself up on a low wall. 'But it happened more than twenty years ago, and you cannot expect me to remember very clearly.'

In those days (said Ganpat) I was quite a young man, and had just been married. I owned several acres of land and, though we were not rich, we were not very poor. When I took my produce to the market, five miles away, I harnessed the bullocks and drove down the dusty village road. I would return home at night.

Every night, I passed a peepul tree, and it was said this tree was haunted. I had never met the ghost and did not believe in him, but his name, I was told, was Bippin, and long ago he had been hanged on the peepul tree by a band of dacoits. Ever since, his ghost had lived in the tree, and was in the habit of pouncing upon any person who resembled a dacoit, and beating him severely. I suppose I must have looked dishonest, for one night Bippin decided to pounce on me. He leapt out of the tree and stood in the middle of the road, blocking the way.

'You, there!' he shouted. 'Get off your cart. I am going to kill you!'

I was, of course, taken aback, but saw no reason why I should obey.

'I have no intention of being killed,' I said. 'Get on the cart yourself!'

'Spoken like a man!' cried Bippin, and he jumped up on the cart beside me. 'But tell me one good reason why I should not kill you?'

'I am not a dacoit,' I replied.

'But you look one. That is the same thing.'

'You would be sorry for it later, if you killed me. I am a poor man, with a wife to support.'

'You have no reason for being poor,' said Bippin, angrily.

'Well, make me rich if you can.'

'So you think I don't have the power to make you rich? Do you defy me to make you rich?'

'Yes,' I said, 'I defy you to make me rich.'

'Then drive on!' cried Bippin. 'I am coming home with you.' I drove the bullock-cart on to the village, with Bippin sitting beside me.

'I have so arranged it,' he said, 'that no one but you will be able to see me. And another thing. I must sleep beside you every night, and no one must know of it. If you tell anyone about me, I'll kill you immediately!'

'Don't worry,' I said. 'I won't tell anyone.'

'Good. I look forward to living with you. It was getting lonely in that peepul tree.'

So Bippin came to live with me, and he slept beside me every night, and we got on very well together. He was as good as his word, and money began to pour in from every conceivable and inconceivable source, until I was in a position to buy more land and cattle. Nobody knew of our association, though of course my friends and relatives wondered where all the money was coming from. At the same time, my wife was rather upset at my refusing to sleep with her at night. I could not very well keep her in the same bed as a ghost, and Bippin was most particular about sleeping beside me. At first, I had told my wife I wasn't well, that I would sleep on the veranda. Then I told her that there was someone after our cows, and I would have to keep an eye on them at night: Bippin and I slept in the barn.

My wife would often spy on me at night, suspecting infidelity, but she always found me lying alone with the cows. Unable to understand my strange behaviour, she mentioned it to her family. They came to me, demanding an explanation.

At the same time, my own relatives were insisting that I tell them the source of my increasing income. Uncles and aunts and distant cousins all descended on me one day, wanting to know where the money was coming from.

'Do you want me to die?' I said, losing patience with them. 'If I tell you the cause of my wealth, I will surely die.'

But they laughed, taking this for a half-hearted excuse; they suspected I was trying to keep everything for myself. My wife's relatives insisted that I had found another woman. Eventually, I grew so exhausted with their demands that I blurted out the truth.

They didn't believe the truth either (who does?), but it gave them something to think and talk about, and they went away for the time being.

But that night, Bippin didn't come to sleep beside me. I was all alone with the cows. And he didn't come the following night. I had been afraid he would kill me while I slept, but it appeared that he had gone his way and left me to my own devices. I was certain that my good fortune had come to an end, and so I went back to sleeping with my wife.

The next time I was driving back to the village from the market, Bippin leapt out of the peepul tree.

'False friend!' he cried, halting the bullocks. 'I gave you everything you wanted, and still you betrayed me!'

'I'm sorry,' I said. 'You can kill me, if you like.'

'No, I cannot kill you,' he said. 'We have been friends for too long. But I will punish you all the same.'

Picking up a stout stick, he struck me three times across the back, until I was bent up double.

'After that,' Ganpat concluded, 'I could never straighten up again and, for over twenty years, I have been a crooked man. My wife left me and went back to her family, and I could no longer work in the fields. I left my village and wandered from one city to another, begging for a living. That is how I came to Pipalnagar, where I decided to remain. People here seem to be more generous than they are in other towns, perhaps because they haven't got so much.'

He looked up at me with a smile, waiting for me to produce the four annas.

'You can't expect me to believe that story,' I said. 'But it was a good invention, so here is your money.'

'No, no!' said Ganpat, backing away and affecting indignation. 'If you don't believe me, keep the money. I would not lie to you for a mere four annas!'

He permitted me to force the coin into his hand, and then went hobbling away, having first wished me a pleasant afternoon.

11

Pitamber is a young lion. A shaggy mane of black hair tumbles down the nape of his neck; his body, though, is naked and hairless, burnt a rich chocolate by the summer sun. His only garment is a pair of knickers. When he pedals his cycle-rickshaw through the streets of Pipalnagar, the muscles of his calves and thighs stand out like lumps of grey iron. He has carried in his rickshaw fat baniyas and their fat wives, and this has given him powerful legs, a strong back and hollow cheeks. His thighs are magnificent, solid muscle, not an ounce of surplus flesh. They look as though they have been carved out of teak.

His face, though, is gaunt and hollow, his eyes set deep in their sockets: but there is a burning intensity about his eyes, and sometimes I wonder if he, too, is tubercular, like many in Pipalnagar. You cannot tell just by looking at a person if he is sick. Sometimes the weak will last for years, while the strong will suddenly collapse and die.

Pitamber has a wife and three children in his village five miles from Pipalnagar. They have a few acres of land on which they grow maize and sugarcane. One day he made me sit in his rickshaw, and we cycled out of the town, along the road to Delhi; then we had to get down and push the rickshaw over a rutted cart-track, until we reached his village.

This visit to Pitamber's village had provided me with an escape route from Pipalnagar. Some weeks later I persuaded Suraj to put aside his tray and his books, and hiring a cycle from a stand near the bus stop (on credit), I seated Suraj in front of me on the cross-bar, and rode out of Pipalnagar.

It was then that I made the amazing discovery that by exerting my legs a little, I could get out of Pipalnagar, and that, except for the cycle-hire, it did not involve any expense or great sacrifice.

It was a hot, sunny morning, and I was perspiring by the time we had gone two miles; but a fresh wind sprang up suddenly, and I could smell rain in the air, though there were no clouds to be seen.

When Suraj began to feel cramped on the saddle-bar, we got down, and walked along the side of the road.

'Let us not go to the village,' said Suraj. 'Let us go where there are no people at all. I am tired of people.'

We pushed the cycle off the road, and took a path through a paddy-field, and then a field of young maize, and in the distance we saw a tree, a crooked tree, growing beside a well.

I do not know the name of that tree. I had never seen one of its kind before. It had a crooked trunk, and crooked branches, and it was clothed in thick, broad crooked leaves, like the leaves on which food is served in the bazaars. In the trunk of the tree was a hole, and when I set my cycle down with a crash, two green parrots flew out of the hole, and went dipping and swerving across the fields.

There was grass around the well, cropped short by grazing cattle, so we sat in the shade of the crooked tree, and Suraj untied the red cloth in which he had brought our food.

We ate our rotis and spiced vegetables, and meanwhile the parrots returned to the tree.

'Let us come here every week,' said Suraj, stretching himself out on the grass and resting his head against my shoulder.

It was a drowsy day, the air humid, and soon Suraj fell asleep. I, too, stretched myself out on the grass, and closed my eyes—but I did not sleep; I was aware instead of a score of different sensations.

I heard a cricket singing in the crooked tree; the cooing of pigeons which dwelt in the walls of the old well; the quiet breathing of Suraj; a rustling in the leaves of the tree; the distant hum of an aeroplane.

I smelt the grass, and the old bricks round the well and the promise of rain.

I felt Suraj's fingers touching my arm, and the sun creeping over my cheek.

I opened my eyes, and I saw the clouds on the horizon, and Suraj still asleep, his arm thrown across his eyes to keep away the glare.

Being thirsty, I went to the well, and putting my shoulders to it, turned the wheel, walking around the well four times, while cool clean water gushed out over the stones and along the channel to the fields.

I drank from one of the trays and the water was sweet with age.

Suraj was sitting up, looking at the sky.

'It is going to rain,' he said. When he had taken his fill of water we pushed the cycle back to the main road and began cycling homewards, but we were still two miles out of Pipalnagar when it began to rain.

A lashing wind swept the rain across our faces, but we exulted in it, and sang at the tops of our voices until we reached the bus stop.

I left the cycle at the hire-shop. Suraj and I ran up the rickety, swaying steps to my room.

Soon there were puddles on the floor, where we had left our soaking clothes, and Suraj was sitting on the bed, a sheet wrapped round his chest.

He became feverish that evening, and I pulled out an old blanket, and covered him with it. I massaged his scalp with mustard oil, and he fell asleep while I did this.

It was dark by then, and the rain had stopped, and the bazaar was lighting up. I curled up at the foot of the bed, and slept for a little while; but at midnight I was woken by the moon shining full in my face; a full moon, shedding its light exclusively on Pipalnagar and peeping and prying into every room, washing the empty streets, silvering the corrugated tin roof.

People are restless tonight, with the moon shining through their windows. Suraj turns restlessly in his sleep. Kamla, having sent away a drunken customer, will be bathing herself, as she always does before she finally sleeps . . . Deep Chand is tossing on his cot, dreaming of electric razors and a plush hair-cutting saloon in the capital, with the Prime Minister as his client. And Seth Govind Ram, unable to sleep because of the accusing moonlight, paces his veranda, worrying about his rent, counting up his assets, and wondering if he should stand for election to the Legislative Assembly.

In the temple the moonlight rests gently on the generous Ganesh, and in the fields Krishna is playing his flute and Radha is singing . . . 'I follow you, devoted . . . How can you deceive me, so tortured by love's fever as I am . . .'

12

In June, the lizards hang listlessly on the walls, scanning their horizon in vain. Insects seldom show up—either the heat has killed them, or they are sleeping and breeding in cracks in the plaster. The lizards wait—and wait . . .

All Pipalnagar is waiting for its release from the oppressive heat of June.

One day clouds loom up on the horizon, growing rapidly into enormous towers. A faint breeze springs up. Soon it is a wind, which brings with it the first raindrops. This is the moment everyone is waiting for. People run out of their chawls and houses to take in the fresh breeze and the scent of those first raindrops on the parched, dusty earth.

Underground, in their cracks and holes, the insects are moving. Termites and white ants, which have been sleeping through the hot season, emerge from their lairs. They have work ahead of them.

Now, on the second or third night of the monsoon, comes the great yearly flight of the insects into the cool brief freedom of the night. Out of every crack, from under the roots of trees, huge winged ants emerge, at first fluttering about heavily, on this the first and last flight of their lives. At night there is only one direction in which they can fly—towards the light; towards the electric bulbs and smoky kerosene lamps that illuminate Pipalnagar.

The street lamp opposite the bus stop, beneath my room, attracts a massive quivering swarm of clumsy termites, which give the impression of one thick, slowly revolving body.

The first frog has arrived and comes hopping on to the balcony to pause beneath the electric bulb. All he has to do is gobble, as the insects fall about him.

This is the hour of the lizards. Now there are rewards for those days of patient waiting. Plying their sticky pink tongues, they devour the insects as fast as they come. For hours they cram their stomachs, knowing that such a feast will not be theirs again for another year.

How wasteful nature is . . . Through the whole hot season the insect world prepares for this flight out of darkness into light, and not one of them survives its freedom.

*

As most of my writing is done at night and much of my sleeping by day, it often happens that at about midnight I put down my pen and go out for a walk. In Pipalnagar this is a pleasant time for a walk, provided you are not taken for a burglar. There is the smell of jasmine in the air, the moonlight shining on sandy stretches of wasteland, and a silence broken only by the hideous bellow of the chowkidar.

This is the person who, employed by the residents of our Mohalla, keeps guard over us at night, and walks the roads calling like a jackal: 'Khabardar!' (Beware) for the benefit of prospective evil-doers. Apart from keeping half the population awake, he is successful in warning thieves of his presence.

The other night, in the course of a midnight stroll I encountered our chowkidar near a dark corner, and wished him a good evening. He leapt into the air like a startled rabbit, and immediately shouted 'Khabardar!' as though this were some magic word that would bring me down on my knees begging for mercy.

'It's quite all right,' I assured him. 'I'm only one of your clients.'

The chowkidar laughed nervously and said he was glad to hear it; he hoped I didn't mind his shouting 'Khabardar' at me, but these were grim times and robbers were on the increase.

I said yes, there were probably quite a few of them at work this very night. Had he ever tried creeping up on them quietly? He might catch a few that way.

But why should he catch them, the chowkidar wanted to know. It was his business to frighten them away. He could do that better by roaring defiantly on the roads than by accosting them on someone's premises—violence must be avoided, if he could help it.

'Besides,' he said, 'the people who live here like me to shout at night. It makes them feel safe, knowing that I am on guard. And if I didn't shout "Khabardar" every few minutes they would think I had fallen asleep, and I would be dismissed.'

This was a logical argument. I asked him what he would do if, by accident, he encountered a gang of thieves. He said he would keep shouting 'Khabardar' until the people came out of their houses to help him. I said I doubted very much if they would come out of their houses, but wished him luck all the same, and continued with my walk.

Every five minutes or so I heard his cry, followed by a 'Khabardar' which grew fainter until the chowkidar had reached the far side of the Mohalla. I thought it would be a good idea to give him a helping hand from my side, so I cupped my hands to my mouth and shouted, 'Khabardar, Khabardar!'

It worked like magic.

Three dark figures scrambled over a neighbouring wall and fled down the empty road. I shouted 'Khabardar' a second time, and they ran faster. Imagine the thieves' confusion when they were met by more 'Khabardars' in front, coming from the chowkidar, and realized that there were now two chowkidars operating in the Mohalla.

*

On those nights when sleep was elusive we left the room and walked for miles around Pipalnagar. It was generally about midnight that we became restless. The walls of the room would give out all the heat they had absorbed during the day, and to lie awake sweating in the dark only gave rise to morbid and depressing thoughts.

In our singlets and pyjamas Suraj and I would walk barefooted through the empty Mohalla, over the cooling brick pavements, until we were out of the bazaar and crossing the Maidan, our feet sinking into the springy dew-fresh grass. The Maidan was broad and spacious, and the star-swept sky seemed to meet each end of the plain.

Then out of the town, through lantana scrub, till we came to the dry river-bed, where we walked amongst rocks and boulders, sitting down occasionally, while great quiet lizards watched us from between the stones.

Across the river-bed fields of maize stretched away for a few miles, until there came a dry region, where thorns and a few bent trees grew, the earth splitting up in jagged cracks like a jigsaw puzzle; and where water had been, the skin was peeling off the earth in great flat pancakes. Dotting the landscape were old abandoned brick kilns, and it was said that thieves met there at nights, in the trenches around the kilns; but we never saw any.

When it rained heavily the hollows filled up with water. Suraj and I came to one of these places to bathe and swim. There was an island in the middle of one of the hollows, and on this small mound stood the ruins of a hut, where a night-watchman once lived and looked after the bricks at night.

We swam out to the island, which was only a few yards away. There was a grassy patch in front of the hut, and here we lay and sunned ourselves in the early morning, until it became too hot. We would oil and massage each other's bodies, and wrestle on the grass.

Though I was heavier than Suraj, and my chest was as sound as a new drum, he had a lot of power in his long arms and legs and often pinioned me about the waist with his bony knees or fastened me with his strong fingers.

Once while we wrestled on the new monsoon grass, I felt his body go tense, as I strained to press his back to the ground. He stiffened, his thigh jerked against me, and his legs began to twitch. I knew that he had a fit coming on, but I was unable to extricate myself from his arms, which gripped me more tightly as the fit took possession of him. Instead of struggling, I lay still, and tried desperately to absorb some of his anguish;

by embracing him, I felt my own body might draw some of the agitation to itself; it was only a strange fancy, but I felt that it made a difference, that by consciously sharing his unconscious condition I was alleviating it. At other times, I have known this same feeling. When Kamla was burning with a fever, I had thought that by taking her in my arms I could draw the fever from her, absorb the heat of her body, transfer to hers the coolness of my own.

Now I pressed against Suraj, and whispered soothingly and lovingly into his ear, though I knew he had no idea what I could be saying; and then when I noticed his mouth working, I thrust my hand in sideways to prevent him from biting his tongue.

But so violent was the convulsion that his teeth bit into the flesh of my palm and ground against my knuckles. I gasped with pain and tried to jerk my hand away, but it was impossible to loosen the grip of his teeth. So I closed my eyes and counted one, two, three, four, five, six, seven—until I felt his body relax again and his jaws give way slowly.

My hand had blood on it, and was trembling: I bound it in a handkerchief, before Suraj came to himself.

We walked back to the town without talking much. He looked depressed and hopeless, though I knew he would be buoyant again before long. I kept my hand concealed beneath my singlet, and he was too dejected to notice this. It was only at night, when he returned from his classes, that he noticed it was bandaged, and then I told him I had slipped on the road, cutting my hand on some broken glass.

13

Rain upon Pipalnagar: and until the rain stops, Pipalnagar is fresh and clean and alive. The children run out of their houses, glorying in their nakedness. They are innocent and unashamed. Older children, by no means innocent, but by all means unashamed, romp through the town, inviting the shocked disapproval of their elders and, presumably, betters.

Before we are ten, we are naked and free and unafraid; after ten, we must cloak our manhood, for we are no longer certain that we are men.

The gutters choke, and the Mohalla becomes a mountain stream, coursing merrily down towards the bus stop. And it is at the bus stop that pandemonium breaks loose; for newly-arrived passengers panic at sight of the sea of mud and rain water that surrounds them on all sides, and about a hundred tongas and cycle-rickshaws try all at once to take care of a score of passengers. Result: only half the passengers find a conveyance, while the other half find themselves knee-deep in Pipalnagar mire.

Pitamber has, of course, succeeded in acquiring as his passenger the most attractive and frightened young woman in the bus, and proceeds to show off his skill and daring by taking her home by the most devious and uncomfortable route, and when she gets her feet covered with mud, wipes them with the seedy red cloth that he ties about his neck.

The rain swirls over the trees and roofs of the town, and the parched earth soaks it up, exuding a fragrance that comes only once in a year, the fragrance of quenched earth, the most exhilarating of all smells.

And in my room, too, I am battling against the elements, for the door will not shut against the breeze, and the rain is sweeping in through the opening and soaking my cot.

When eventually I succeed in barricading the floor, I find the roof leaking, and the water trickling down the walls, obliterating the dusty designs I have made on the plaster with my foot. I place a tin here and a mug there, and then, satisfied that everything is under control, sit on my cot and watch the roof-tops through my window.

But there is a loud banging on the door. It flies open with the pressure, and there is Suraj, standing on the threshold, shaking himself like a wet dog. Coming in, he strips off all his clothes, and then he dries himself with a torn threadbare towel, and sits shivering on the bed while I make frantic efforts to close the door again.

'You are cold, Suraj, I will make you some tea.'

He nods, forgetting to smile for once, and I know his mind is elsewhere, in one of a thousand places and all of them dreams.

When I have got the fire going, and placed the kettle on the red hot coals, I sit down beside Suraj and put my arm around his bony shoulders and dream a little with him.

'One day I will write a book,' I tell him. 'Not a murder story, but a real book, about real people. Perhaps it will be about you and me and Pipalnagar. And then we will break away from Pipalnagar, fly away like eagles, and our troubles will be over and fresh new troubles will begin. I do not mind difficulties, as long as they are new difficulties.'

'First I must pass my exams,' said Suraj. 'Without a certificate one can do nothing, go nowhere.'

'Who taught you such nonsense? While you are preparing for your exams, I will be writing my book. That's it! I will start tonight. It is an auspicious night, the first night of the monsoon. Let us start tonight.'

And by the time we had drunk our tea it was evening and growing dark. The light did not come on; a tree must have fallen across the wires. So I lit a candle and placed it on the window-sill (the rain and wind had ceased), and while the candle spluttered in the steady stillness, Suraj opened his books and with one hand on a book, and the other playing with his toes—this helped him to read—he began his studies.

I took the ink down from the shelf, and finding the bottle empty, added a little rain-water to it from one of the mugs. I sat down beside Suraj and began to write; but the pen was no good, and made blotches all over and I didn't really know what to write about, though I was full of writing just then.

So I began to look at Suraj instead; at his eyes, hidden in the shadows, his hands in the candle light; and felt his breathing and the slight movement of his lips as he read shortly to himself.

*

A gust of wind came through the window, and the candle went out.

I swore softly in Punjabi.

'Never mind,' said Suraj, 'I was tired of reading.'

'But I was writing.'

'Your book?'

'No, a letter . . .'

'I have never known you to write letters, except to publishers asking them for money. To whom were you writing?'

'To you,' I said. 'And I will send you the letter one day, perhaps when we are no longer together.'

'I will wait for it, then. I will not read it now.'

14

At ten o'clock on a wet night Pipalnagar had its first earthquake in thirty years. It lasted exactly five seconds. A low, ominous rumble was followed by a few quick shudders, and the water surahi jumped off the window-ledge and crashed on the floor.

By the time Suraj and I had tumbled out of the room, the shock was over; but panic prevailed, and the entire population of the Mohalla was out in the street. One old man of seventy leapt from a first floor balcony and broke his neck; a large crowd had gathered round his body. Several women had fainted. On the other hand, many were shrieking and running about. Only a few days back astrologers had predicted the end of the world, and everyone was convinced that this was only the first of a series of earthquakes.

At temples and other places of worship prayer meetings were held. People moved about the street, pointing out the cracks that had appeared in their houses. Some of these cracks had, of course, been there for years, and were only now being discovered.

At midnight, men and women were still about; and, as though to justify their prudence, another, milder tremor made itself felt. The roof of an old house, weakened by many heavy monsoons, was encouraged to give way, and fell with a suitably awe-inspiring crash. Fortunately no one was beneath it. Everyone was soaking wet by now, as the rain had come down harder, but no one dared venture indoors, especially after a roof had fallen in.

Worse still, the electricity failed and the entire Mohalla plunged into darkness. People huddled together, fearing the worst, while the rain came down incessantly.

'More people will die of pneumonia than earthquake,' observed Suraj. 'Let's go for a walk, it is better than standing about doing nothing.'

We rolled up our pyjamas and went splashing through the puddles. On the outskirts of the town we met Pitamber dancing in the middle of the road. He was very merry, and quite drunk.

'Why are you dancing in the road?' I asked.

'Because I am happy, that's why,' said Pitamber.

'And what makes you so happy, my friend?'

'Because I am dancing in the road,' he replied.

We began walking home again. The rain had stopped. There was a break in the clouds and a pale moon appeared. The neem trees gave out a strong, sweet smell.

There were no more tremors that night. When we got back to the Mohalla, the sky was lighter, and people were beginning to move into their houses again.

*

We lay on our island, in the shade of a thorn bush, watching a pair of sarus cranes on the opposite bank prancing and capering around each other; tall, stork-like birds, with naked red heads and long red legs.

'We might be saruses in some future life,' I said.

'I hope so,' said Suraj. 'Even if it means being born on a lower level. I would like to be a beautiful white bird. I am tired of being a man, but I do not want to leave the world altogether. It is very lovely, sometimes.'

'I would like to be a sacred bird,' I said. 'I don't wish to be shot at.'

'Aren't saruses sacred? Look how they enjoy themselves.'

'They are making love. That is their principal occupation apart from feeding themselves. And they are so devoted to each other that if one bird is killed the other will haunt the scene for weeks, calling distractedly. They have even been known to pine away and die of grief. That's why they are held in such affection by people in villages.'

'So many birds are sacred.'

We saw a blue jay swoop down from a tree—a flash of blue— and carry off a grasshopper.

'Both the blue jay and Lord Siva are called Nilkanth. Siva has a blue throat, like the blue jay, because out of compassion for the human race he swallowed a deadly poison which was meant to destroy the world. He kept the poison in his throat and would not let it go any further.'

'Are squirrels sacred?' asked Suraj, curiously watching one fumbling with a piece of bread which we had thrown away.

'Krishna loved them. He would take them in his arms and stroke them with his long, gentle fingers. That is why they have four dark lines down their backs from head to tail. Krishna was very dark-skinned, and the lines are the marks of his fingers.'

'We should be gentle to animals . . . Why do we kill so many of them?'

'It is not so important that we do not kill them—it is important that we respect them. We must acknowledge their right to live on this earth. Everywhere, birds and animals are finding it more difficult to survive, because we are destroying their homes. They have to keep moving as the trees and the green grass keep disappearing.'

*

Flowers in Pipalnagar—do they exist?

I have known flowers in poetry, and as a child I knew a garden in Lucknow where there were fields of flowers, and another garden where only roses grew. In the fields round Pipalnagar I have seen dandelions that evaporate when you breathe on them, and sometimes a yellow buttercup nestling among thistles. But in our Mohalla, there are no flowers except one. This is a marigold growing out of a crack in my balcony.

I have removed the plaster from the base of the plant, and filled in a little earth which I water every morning. The plant is healthy, and sometimes it produces a little orange marigold, which I pluck and give away before it dies.

Sometimes Suraj keeps the flower in his tray, among the combs and scent bottles and buttons that he sells. Sometimes he offers the flower to a passing child—to a girl who runs away; or it might be a boy who tears the flower to shreds. Some children keep it; others give flowers to Suraj when he passes their houses.

Suraj has a flute which he plays whenever he is tired of going from house to house.

He will sit beneath a shady banyan or peepul, put his tray aside, and take out his flute. The haunting little notes travel down the road in the afternoon stillness, and children come to sit beside him and listen to the flute music. They are very quiet when he plays, because there is a little sadness about his music, and children especially can sense that sadness.

Suraj has made flutes out of pieces of bamboo; but he never sells them, he gives them away to the children he likes. He will sell anything, but not his flutes.

Sometimes Suraj plays his flutes at night, when I am lying awake on the cot, unable to sleep; and even when I fall asleep, the flute is playing in my dreams. Sometimes he brings it with him to the crooked tree, and plays it for the benefit of the birds; but the parrots only make harsh noises and fly away.

Once, when Suraj was playing his flute to a group of children, he had a fit. The flute fell from his hands, and he began to roll about in the dust on the roadside. The children were frightened and ran away.

But they did not stay away for long. The next time they heard the flute play, they came to listen as usual.

15

As Suraj and I walked over a hill near the limestone quarries, past the shacks of the Bihari labourers, we met a funeral procession on its way to the cremation ground. Suraj placed his hand on my arm and asked me to wait until the procession had passed. At the same time a cyclist dismounted and stood at the side of the road. Others hurried on, without glancing at the little procession.

'I was taught to respect the dead in this way,' said Suraj. 'Even if you do not respect a man in life, you should respect him in death. The body is unimportant, but we should honour it out of respect for the man's mind.'

'It is a good custom,' I said.

'It must be difficult to live on after one you have loved has died.'

'But you do,' I said, reminded of my mother. 'And if a love is strong, I cannot see its end . . . It cannot end in death, I feel . . . Even physically, you would exist for me somehow.'

*

He was asleep when I returned late at night from a card-game in which I had lost fifty rupees. I was a little drunk, and when I tripped near the doorway, he woke up; and though he did not open his eyes, I felt he was looking at me.

I felt very guilty and ashamed, because he had been ill that day, and I had forgotten it. Now there was no point in saying I was sorry. Drunkenness is really a vice, because it degrades a man, and humiliates him.

Prostitution is degrading, but a prostitute can still keep her dignity; thieving is degrading according to the character of the theft; begging is degrading but it is not as undignified as drunkenness. In all our vices we are aware of our degradation; but in drunkenness we lose our pride, our heads, and, above all, our natural dignity. We become so obviously and helplessly 'human', that we lose our glorious animal identity.

I sat down at the side of the bed, and bending over Suraj, whispered, 'I got drunk and lost fifty rupees, what am I to do about it?'

He smiled, but still he didn't open his eyes, and I kicked off my sandals and pulled off my shirt and lay down across the foot of the bed. He was still burning with fever, I could feel it radiating through the sheet.

We were silent for a long time, and I didn't know if he was awake or asleep; so I pressed his foot and said, 'I'm sorry,' but he was asleep now, and did not hear me.

*

Moonlight.

Pipalnagar looks clean in the moonlight, and my thoughts are different from my daytime thoughts.

The streets are empty, and the moon probes the alleyways, and there is a silver dustbin, and even the slush and the puddles near the bus stop shimmer and glisten.

Kisses in the moonlight. Hungry kisses. The shudder of bodies clinging to each other on the moonswept floor.

A drunken quarrel in the street. Voices rise and fall. The chowkidar waits for the trouble to pass, and then patrols the street once more, banging the lathi on the pavement.

Kamla asleep. She sleeps like an angel. I go downstairs and walk in the moonlight. I meet Suraj coming home, his books under his arm; he has been studying late with Aziz, who keeps a junk shop near the station. Their exams are only a month off. I am confident that Suraj will be successful; I am only afraid that he will work himself to a standstill; with his weak chest and the uncertainty of his fits, he should not walk all day and read all night.

When I wake in the early hours of the morning and Kamla stirs beside me in her sleep (her hair so laden with perfume that my own sleep has been fitful and disturbed), Suraj is still squatting on the floor, reading by the light of the kerosene lamp.

And even when he has finished reading he does not sleep, but asks me to walk with him before the sun rises, and, as women were not made to get up before the sun, we leave Kamla stretched out on the cot, relaxed and languid; small breasts and a boy's waist; her hair tumbling about the pillow; her mouth slightly apart, her lips still swollen and bruised with kisses.

16

It was Lord Krishna's birthday, and the rain came down as heavily as it must have done the day Krishna was born in Brindaban. Krishna is the best beloved of all the gods. Young mothers laugh and weep as they read or hear about the pranks of his childhood; young men pray to be as tall and strong as Krishna was when he killed Kamsa's elephant and Kamsa's wrestlers; young girls dream of a lover as daring as Krishna to carry them off like Rukmani in a war chariot; grown up men envy the wisdom and statesmanship with which he managed the affairs of his kingdom.

The rain came suddenly and took everyone by surprise. In a few seconds, people were drenched to the skin, and within ten minutes the Mohalla was completely flooded. The temple tank overflowed, the railway lines disappeared, and the old wall near the bus stop shivered and fell silently, the noise of the collapse drowned by the rain.

Those whose beard had not yet appeared enjoyed themselves immensely. Children shrieked with excitement, and five naked young men with a dancing bear cavorted in the middle of the vegetable market.

Wading knee-deep down the road, I saw roadside vendors salvaging what they could. Plastic toys, cabbages and utensils floated away and were seized upon by urchins. The water had risen to the level of the shop-fronts, and the floors were awash. Aziz was afloat in his junk shop. Deep Chand, Ramu and a customer were using buckets to bail the water out of their premises. Pitamber churned through the stream in his cycle-rickshaw, offering free lifts to the women in the bazaar with their saris held high above their knees.

The rain stopped as suddenly as it had begun. The sun came out. The water began to find an outlet, flooding other low-lying areas, and a paper-boat came sailing between my legs.

*

'When did you last go out of Pipalnagar?' I asked Suraj. 'I mean far out, to another part of the country?'

'Not since I came here,' he said. 'I have never had the funds. And you?'

'I don't remember. I have been stagnating in Pipalnagar for five years without a break. I would like to see the hills again. Once, when I was a child, my parents took me to the hills. I remember them vividly—pine trees, the wind at night, men carrying loads of wood up the steep mountain paths—yes, I would like to see the hills again . . .'

'I have never seen them,' said Suraj.

'How strange! I don't think that a man can be complete until he has lived in the hills. Of course we are never complete, but there is something about a mountain that adds a new dimension to life. The change in air and altitude makes one think and feel and act differently. Suraj, we must go to the hills! This is the time to go. Let's get away from this insufferable heat, from these drains and smells and noises—even if it is only for a few days . . .'

'But my exams are only a few weeks off.'

'Good. The change will help. Bring your books along. You will study much better there. You will feel better. I can guarantee that you will not have a single fit all the time we are away!'

I was carried away in a flood of enthusiasm. I waved my arms about and described the splendour of the sun rising—or setting—behind Nanda Devi, and talked about the book I could write if I stayed a few weeks in the hills.

'But what about money?' interrupted Suraj, breaking in on my oration. 'How do we go there?'

'Money?' I said contemptuously. 'Money?' I said again, more respectfully. And then doubtfully, 'Money.'

'Yes, money,' I muttered to myself, and sat down on the string cot, suddenly deflated and discouraged.

Suraj burst into laughter.

'What are you laughing about?' I hissed.

'I can't help it,' he said, holding his sides with mirth. 'It's your face. One minute it was broad with smiles, now it is long and mournful, like the face of a horse.'

'We'll get money!' I shouted, springing up again. 'How much do we need—two hundred, five hundred—it's easy! My gold ring can be pawned. On our return we shall retrieve it. The book will see to that.'

I was never to see my ring again, but that did not matter. We managed to raise a hundred rupees, and with it we prepared ourselves feverishly for our journey, afraid that at the last moment something would prevent us from going.

We were to travel by train to the railway terminus, a night's journey, then take the bus. Though we hoped to be away for at least a week, our funds did not in fact last more than four days.

We locked our room, left the key with Kamla, and asked Deep Chand to keep an eye on both her and our things.

In the train that night Suraj had a mild fit. It helped reduce the numbers in our compartment. Some, thinking he suffered from a communicable disease, took themselves and their belongings elsewhere; others, used to living with illness, took no notice. But Suraj was not to have any more fits until we returned to Pipalnagar.

We slept fitfully that night, continually shifting our positions on the hard bench of the third-class compartment; Suraj with his head against my shoulder, I with my feet on my bedding roll. Above us, a Sikh farmer slept vigorously, his healthy snores reverberating through the compartment. A woman with her brood of four or five children occupied the bunk opposite; they had knocked over their earthen surahi, smashing it and flooding the compartment. Two young men in the corner played cards and exchanged lewd jokes. No general companionship was at all evident, but whenever the train drew into a station everyone cooperated in trying to prevent people on the outside from entering the already crowded compartment; and if someone did manage to get in—usually by crawling through a window—he would fall in with the same policy of keeping others out.

We woke in the early hours of the morning and looked out of the window at the changing landscape. It was so long since I had seen trees—not trees singly or in clumps, but forests of trees, thick and dark and broody, commencing at the railway tracks and stretching away to the foothills. Trees full of birds and monkeys; and in the forest clearing we saw a deer, it's head raised, scenting the wind.

17

There were many small hotels in the little town that straddled two or three hills; but Suraj and I went to a dharamsala where we were given a small room overlooking the valley. We did not spend much time there. There were too many hills and streams and trees inviting us on all sides; it seemed as though they had been waiting all those years for our arrival. Each tree has an individuality of its own—perhaps more individuality than a man—and if you look at a tree with a personal eye, it will give you something of itself, something deep and personal; its smell, its sap, its depth and wisdom.

So we mingled with the trees. We felt and understood the dignity of the pine, the weariness of the willow, the resignation of the oak. The blossoms had fallen from the plum and apricot trees, and the branches were bare, touched with the light green of new foliage. Pine needles made the ground soft and slippery, and we went sliding downhill on our bottoms.

Then we took paper and pencil and some mangoes, and went among some rocks, and there I wrote odd things that came into my head, about the hills and the sounds we heard.

The silence of the mountains was accentuated by the occasional sounds around us—a shepherd boy shouting to his mate, a girl singing to her cattle, the jingle of cow bells, a woman pounding clothes on a flat stone . . . Then, when these sounds stopped, there were quieter, subtler sounds— the singing of crickets, whistling of anonymous birds, the wind soughing in the pine trees.

It was hot in the sun, until a cloud came over, and then it was suddenly cool, and our shirts flapped against us in the breeze.

The hills went striding away into the distance. The nearest hill was covered with oak and pine, the next was brown and naked and topped with a white temple, like a candle on a fruit-cake. The furthest hill was a misty blue.

18

The 'season' as they called it, was just beginning in the hills. Those who had money came to the hill-station for a few weeks, to parade up and down the Mall in a variety of costumes ranging from formal dinner jackets to cowboy jeans. There were the Anglicized elite, models of English gentry, and there was the younger set, imitating western youth as depicted in films and glossy magazines. Suraj and I felt out of place walking down the Mall in kameez and pyjamas; we were foreigners on our own soil. Were these really Indians exhibiting themselves, or were they ghastly caricatures of the West?

The town itself had gone to seed. English houses and cottages, built by unimaginative Victorians to last perhaps fifty years, were now over a hundred years old, all in a state of immediate collapse. No one repaired them, no one tore them down. Some had been built to look like Swiss chateaux, others like *Arabian Nights* castles, most like homely English cottages—all were out of place, incongruous oddities desecrating a majestic mountain.

Though the Sahibs had gone long ago, coolie-drawn rickshaws still plied the steep roads, transporting portly Bombay and Delhi businessmen and their shrill, quarrelsome wives from one end of the hill-station to the other. It was as though a community of wealthy Indians had colonized an abandoned English colony, and had gone native, adopting English clothes and attitudes.

*

A lonely place on a steep slope, hidden by a thicket of oaks through which the sun filtered warmly. We lay on crisp dry oak leaves, while a cool breeze fanned our naked bodies.

I wondered at the frail beauty of Suraj's body, at the transient beauty of all flesh, the vehicle of our consciousness. I thought of Kamla's body—firm, supple, economical, in spite of the indignities to which it had been put; of the body of a child, soft and warm and throbbing with vigour; the bodies of pot-bellied glandular males; and bodies bent and deformed and eaten away . . . The armours of our consciousness, every hair from the head to the genitals a live and beautiful thing . . .

But let me not confine myself to the few years between this birth and this death—which is, after all, only the period I can remember well . . . I believe in the death of flesh, but not in the end of living.

When, at the age of six, I saw my first mountain, it did not astonish me; it was something new and exhilarating, but all the same I felt I had known mountains before. Trees and flowers and rivers were not strange things. I had lived with them, too. In new places, new faces, we see the familiar. Even as children we are old in experience. We are not conscious of a beginning, only of an eternity.

Death must be an interval, a rest for a tired and misused body, which has to be destroyed before it can be renewed. But consciousness is a continuing thing. Our very thoughts have an existence of their own. Are we so unimaginative as to presume that life is confined to the shells that are our bodies? Science and religion have not even touched upon the mysteries of our existence.

In moments of rare intimacy, for instance, two people are of one mind and one body, speaking only in thoughts, brilliantly aware of each other.

I have felt this way about Suraj even when he is far away; his thoughts hover about me, as they do now.

He lies beside me with his eyes closed and his head turned away, but all the time we are talking, talking, talking . . .

*

To a temple on the spur of a hill. Scrambling down a slippery hillside, getting caught in thorny thickets, among sharp rocks; along a dry water-course, where we saw the skeleton of a jungle-cat, its long, sharp teeth still in perfect condition.

A footpath, winding round the hill to the temple; a forest of silver oaks shimmering in the breeze. Cool, sweet water bubbling out of the mountain side, the sweetest, most delicious water I have ever tasted, coming through rocks and ferns and green grasses.

Then up, up, up the steep mountain, where long-fingered cacti point to the sloping sky and pebbles go tumbling into the valley below. A giant langur, with a five-foot long tail, leaps from tree to jutting boulder, anxious lest we invade its domain among the unattended peach trees.

On top of the hill, a little mound of stones and a small cross. I wondered what lonely, romantic foreigner, so different from his countrymen, could have been buried here, where sky and mountain meet.

19

Though we had lost weight in the hills, through climbing and riding, the good clean air had sweetened our blood, and we felt like spartans on our return to Pipalnagar.

That Suraj was gaining in strength I knew from the way he pinned me down when we wrestled on the sand near the old brick-kilns. It was no longer necessary for me to yield a little to him. Though his fits still occurred from time to time as they would continue to do—the anxiety and the death had gone from his eyes.

Suraj passed his examinations. We never doubted that he would. Still, neither of us could sleep the night before the results appeared. We lay together in the dark and spoke of many things—of living and dying, and the reason for all striving—we asked each other the same questions that thousands have asked themselves—and like those thousands, we had no answers; we could not even comfort ourselves with religion, because God eluded us.

Only once had I felt the presence of God. I woke one morning, and finding Suraj asleep beside me, was overcome by a tremendous happiness, and kept saying, 'Thank you, God, thank you for giving me Suraj . . .'

The newspapers came with the first bus, at six in the morning. A small crowd of students had gathered at the bus stop, joking with each other and hiding their nervous excitement with a hearty show of indifference.

There were not many passengers on the first bus, and there was a mad grab for the newspapers as the bundle landed with a thud on the pavement. Within half an hour the newsboy had sold all his copies. It was the only day of the year when he had a really substantial sale.

Suraj did not go down to meet the bus, but I did. I was more nervous than he, I think. And I ran my eye down the long columns of roll numbers so fast that I missed his number the first time. I began again, in a panic, then found it at the top of the list, among the successful ones.

I looked up at Suraj who was standing on the balcony of my room, and he could tell from my face that he had passed, and he smiled down at me. I joined him on the balcony, and we looked down at the other boys comparing newspapers, some of them exultant, some resigned; a few still hopeful, still studying the columns of roll numbers—each number representing a year's concentration on dull, ill-written text books.

Those who had failed had nothing to be ashamed of. They had failed through sheer boredom.

*

I had been called to Delhi for an interview, and I needed a shirt. The few I possessed were either torn at the shoulders or frayed at the collars. I knew writers and artists were not expected to dress very well, but I felt I was not in a position to indulge in eccentricities. Why display my poverty to an editor, of all people.

Where was I to get a shirt? Suraj generally wore an old red-striped T-shirt; he washed it every second evening, and by morning it was dry and ready to wear again; but it was tight even for him. What I needed was something white, something respectable.

I went to Deep Chand. He had a collection of shirts. He was only too glad to lend me one. But they were all brightly coloured things—yellow and purple and pink. They would not impress an editor. No editor could possibly take a liking to an author who wore a pink shirt. They looked fine on Deep Chand when he was cutting people's hair.

Pitamber was also unproductive; he had only someone's pyjama coat to offer.

In desperation, I went to Kamla.

'A shirt?' she said. 'I'll soon get a shirt for you. Why didn't you ask me before? I'll have it ready for you in the morning.'

And not only did she produce a shirt next morning, but a pair of silver cuff-links as well.

'Whose are these?' I asked.

'One of my visitors', she replied with a shrug. 'He was about your size. As he was quite drunk when he went home, he did not realize that I had kept his shirt. He had removed it to show me his muscles, as I kept telling him he hadn't any to show. Not where it really mattered.'

I laughed so much that my belly ached (laughing on a half empty stomach is painful) and kissed the palms of Kamla's hands and told her she was wonderful.

*

Freedom.

The moment the bus was out of Pipalnagar, and the fields opened out on all sides, I knew I was free; that I had always been free; held back only by my own weakness, lacking the impulse and the imagination to break away from an existence that had become habitual for years.

And all I had to do was sit in a bus and go somewhere.

Only by leaving Pipalnagar could I help Suraj. Brooding in my room, I was no good to anyone.

I sat near the open window of the bus and let the cool breeze freshen my face. Herons and snipe waded among the lotus on flat green ponds; blue jays swooped around the telegraph poles; and children jumped naked into the canals that wound through the fields.

Because I was happy, it seemed that everyone else was happy—the driver, the conductor, the passengers, the farmers in their fields, on their bullock-carts. When two women began quarrelling over a coat behind me, I intervened, and with tact and sweetness soothed their tempers. Then I took a child on my knee, and pointed out camels and buffaloes and vultures and pariah-dogs.

And six hours later the bus crossed the swollen river Yamuna, passed under the giant red walls of the fort built by Shahjahan, and entered the old city of Delhi.

20

The editor of the Urdu weekly had written asking me if I would care to be his literary editor; he was familiar with some of my earlier work—poems and stories—and had heard that my circumstances and the quality of my work had deteriorated. Though he did not promise me a job, and did not offer to pay my fare to Delhi, or give me any idea of what my salary might be, there was the offer and there was the chance—an opportunity to escape, to enter the world of the living, to write, to read, to explore.

On my second night in Delhi I wrote to Suraj from the station waiting room, resting the pad on my knee as I sat alone with my suitcase in one corner of the crowded room. Women chattered amongst themselves, or slept silently, children wandered about on the platform outside, babies cried or searched for their mothers' breasts.

*

Dear Suraj:

It is strange to be in a city again, after so many years of Pipalnagar. It is a little frightening, too. You suffer a loss of identity, as you feel your way through the indifferent crowds in Chandni Chowk late in the evening; you are an alien amongst the Westernized who frequent the restaurants and shops at Connaught Place; a stranger amongst one's fellow refugees who have grown prosperous now and live in the flat treeless colonies that have mushroomed around the city. It is only when I am near an old tomb or in the garden of a long-forgotten king, that I become conscious of my identity again.

I wish you had accompanied me. That would have made this an exciting, not an intimidating experience!

Anyway, I shall see you in a day or two. I think I have the job. I saw my editor this morning. He is from Hyderabad. Just imagine the vastness of our country, that it should take almost half a lifetime for a north Indian to meet a south Indian for the first time in his life.

I don't think my editor is very fond of north Indians, judging from some of his remarks about Punjabi traders and taxi-drivers in Delhi; but he liked what he called my unconventionality (I don't know if he meant my work or myself). I said I thought he was the unconventional one. This always pleases, and he asked me what salary I would expect if he offered me a position on his staff. I said three hundred; he said he might not manage to get me so much, but if they offered me one-fifty, would I accept? I said I would think about it and let him know the next day.

Now I am cursing myself for not having accepted it there and then; but I did not want to appear too eager or desperate, and I must not give the impression that a job is indispensable to me. I told him that I had actually come to Delhi to do some research for a book I intended writing about the city. He asked me the title, and I thought quickly and said, 'Delhi Is Still Far' Nizamuddin's comment when told that Tughlaq Shah was marching to Delhi—and he was suitably impressed.

Thinking about it now, perhaps it would be a good idea to do a book about Delhi—its cities and kings, poets and musicians . . . I walked the streets all day, wandering through the bazaars, down the wide shady roads of the capital, resting under the jamun trees near Humayun's tomb, and thinking all the time of what you and I can do here; and while I wander about Delhi, you must be wandering around Pipalnagar, with that wonderful tray of yours . . .

*

Chandni Chowk has not changed in character even if its face has a different look. It is still the heart of Delhi, still throbbing with vitality—more so perhaps, with the advent of the enterprising Punjabi. The old buildings and landmarks are still there, the lanes and alleys are as tortuous and mysterious as ever. Travellers and cloth merchants and sweetmeats-sellers may have changed name and character, but their professions have not given place to new ones. And if on a Sunday the shops must close, they may spill out on the pavement and across the tramlines—toys, silks, cottons, glassware, china, basket-work, furniture, carpets, perfumes—

it is as busy as on any market-day and the competition is louder and more fierce.

In front of the Town Hall the statue of Queen Victoria frowns upon the populace, as ugly as all statues, flecked with pigeon droppings. The pigeons, hundreds of them sit on the railings and the telegraph wires, their drowsy murmuring muted by the sounds of the street, the cries of vendors and tonga drivers and the rattle of the tram.

The tram is a museum-piece. I don't think it has been replaced since it was first installed over fifty years ago. It crawls along the crowded thoroughfare, clanging at an impatient five miles an hour, bursting at the seams with its load of people, while urchins hang on by their toes and eyebrows.

An ash-smeared ascetic sits at the side of the road, and cooks himself a meal; a juggler is causing a traffic jam; a man has a lotus tattooed on his forearm. From the balcony of the Sonehri the invader Nadir Shah watched the slaughter of Delhi's citizens. I walk down the Dariba, famed street of the Silversmiths, and find myself at the steps of the Jama Masjid, surrounded by bicycle shops, junk shops, fish shops, bird shops, and fat goats ready for slaughter. Cities and palaces have risen and fallen on the plains of Delhi, but Chandni Chowk is indestructible, the heart of both old and new.

*

All night long I hear the shunting and whistling of engines, and like a child I conjure up visions of places with sweet names like Kumbekonam, Krishnagiri, Mahabalipuram and Polonnarurawa; dreams of palm-fringed beaches and inland lagoons; of the echoing chambers of some deserted city, red sandstone and white marble; of temples in the sun, and elephants crossing wide slow-moving rivers . . .

I have a sudden desire to travel. Right now I feel I could travel forever through my country; I don't think I will ever tire of it. Ours is a land of many people, many races; their diversity gives it colour and character. For all Indians to be alike would be as dull as for all sexes to be the same, or for all humans to be normal. In Delhi, too, there is a richness of race, though the Punjabi predominates—in shops, taxis, motor workshops and carpenters' sheds. But in the old city there are still many Muslims following traditional trades— bakers, butchers, painters, makers of toys and kites. South Indians have filled our offices; Rajasthanis move dexterously along the scaffolding of new buildings springing up everywhere; and in the surrounding countryside nomadic Gujjars still graze their cattle, while settled villagers find their lands selected for trails of new tubewells, pumps, fertilizers and ploughs.

*

The city wakes early. The hour before sunrise is the only time when it is possible to exercise. Once the sun is up, people must take refuge beneath fans or in the shade of jamun and neem trees. September in Delhi is sultry and humid, relieved only by an occasional monsoon downpour. In the old city there is always the danger of cholera; in the new capital, people fall ill from sitting too long in air-conditioned cinemas and restaurants.

At noon the streets are almost empty; but early in the morning everyone is about, young and old, shopkeeper and clerk, taxi driver and shoeshine boy, flooding the maidans and open spaces in their vests and underwear. Some sprint around the maidans; some walk briskly down the streets, swinging their arms like soldiers; young men wrestle, or play volley-ball or kabaddi; others squat on their haunches, some stand on their heads; some pray, facing the sun; some study books, mumbling to themselves, or make speeches to vast, invisible audiences; scrub their teeth with neem twigs, bathe at public taps, wash clothes, tie dhotis or turbans and go about their business.

The sun is up, clerks are asleep with their feet up at their desks, government employees drink innumerable cups of tea, and the machinery of bureaucracy and civilization runs on as smoothly as ever.

Soon I will be part of all this.

21

Suraj was on the platform when the Pipalnagar Express steamed into the station in the early hours of a warm late September morning. I wanted to shout to him from the carriage window, to tell him that everything was well, that the world was wonderful, and that I loved him and the world and everything in it.

But I couldn't say anything until we had left the station and I was drinking hot tea on the string-bed in our room.

'It is three hundred a month,' I said, 'but we should be able to manage on that, if we are careful. And now that you have done your matriculation, you will be able to join the Polytechnic. So we will both be busy. And when we are not working, we shall have all Delhi to explore. It will be better in the city. One should live either in a city or in a village. In a village, everyone knows you intimately. In a city, no one has the slightest interest in you. But in a town like Pipalnagar, everyone knows you, nobody loves you; when you die, you are forgotten; while you live, you are only a subject for malicious conversation. Poor Pipalnagar . . . Will you be sorry to leave the place, Suraj?'

'Yes, I will be sorry. This is where I have lived.'

'This is where I've existed. I only began to live when I realized I could leave the place.'

'When we went to the hills?'

'When I met you.'

'How did I change anything? I am still an additional burden.'

'You have made me aware of who and what I am.'

'I don't understand.'

'I don't want you to. That would spoil it.'

*

There was no rent to be paid before we left, as Seth Govind Ram's Munshi had taken it in advance, and there were five days to go before the end of the month; there was little chance of the balance being returned to us.

Deep Chand was happy to know that we were leaving. 'I shall follow you soon,' he said. 'There is money to be made in Delhi, cutting hair. Why, even girls are beginning to keep short hair. I shall keep a special saloon for ladies, which Ramu can attend. Women feel safe with him, he looks so pretty and innocent.'

Ramu winked at me in the mirror. I could not imagine anyone less innocent. Girls going to school and college still complained that he harassed them and threatened to remove their pigtails with his razor.

The snip of Deep Chand's scissors lulled me to sleep as I sat in his chair; his fingers beat a rhythmic tattoo on my scalp; his razor caressed by cheeks. It was my last shave, and Deep Chand did not charge me anything. I promised to write to him as soon as I had settled down in Delhi.

*

Kamla had gone home for a few days. Her village was about five miles from Pipalnagar in the opposite direction to Pitamber's, among the mustard and wheat fields that sloped down to the banks of the little water-course. I worked my way downstream until I came to the fields.

I waited behind some trees on the outskirts of the village until I saw her playing with a little boy; I whistled and stepped out of the trees, but when she saw me she motioned me back, and took the child into one of the small mud houses.

I waited amongst the sal trees until I heard footsteps a short distance away.

'Where are you?' I called, but received no answer. I walked in the direction of the footsteps, and found a small path going through the trees. After a short distance the path turned to meet a stream, and Kamla was waiting there.

'Why didn't you wait for me?' I asked.

'I wanted to see if you could follow me.'

'Well, I am good at it.' I said, sitting down beside her on the bank of the stream. The water was no more than ankle-deep, cool and clear. I took off my shoes, rolled up my trousers, and put my feet in the water. Kamla was barefooted, and so she had to tuck up her sari a little, before slipping her feet in.

With my feet I churned up the mud at the bottom of the stream. As the mud subsided, I saw her face reflected in the water; and looking up at her again, into her dark eyes, I wanted to care for her and protect her, I wanted to take her away from Pipalnagar; I wanted her to live like other people. Of course, I had forgotten all about my poor finances.

I kissed the tips of her fingers, then her neck. She ran her fingers through my hair. The rain began splatting down and Kamla said, 'Let us go.'

We set off. Soon the rain began pelting down. Kamla shook herself free and we dashed for cover. She was breathing heavily and I kissed her again. Kamla's hair came loose and streamed down her body. We had to hop over pools, and avoid the soft mud. And then I thought she was crying, but I wasn't sure, it might have been the raindrops on her cheeks, and her heavy breathing.

'Come with me,' I said. 'Come away from Pipalnagar.'

She smiled.

'Why can't you come?'

'Because you really do not want me to. For you, a woman would only be a liability. You are free like birds, you and Suraj, you can go where you like and do as you like. I cannot help you in any way. And what use is a woman to a man if she cannot help him? I have helped you to pass your time in Pipalnagar. That is something. I am part of this place. Neither Pipalnagar nor I can change. But you can, simply by going away.'

'Will you come later, once I have started making a living in Delhi?'

'I am married, it is as simple as that . . .'

'If it is that simple, you can come.'

'I have to think of my parents, you know. It would ruin them if I ran away.'

'Yes, but they do not care if they have broken your heart.'

She shrugged and looked away towards the village. 'I am not so unhappy. He is an old fool, my husband, and I get some fun out of teasing him. He will die one day, and so will the Seth, and then I will be free.'

'Will you?'

'Why not? And anyway, you can always come to see me, and nobody will be made unhappy by it.'

I felt sad and frustrated but I couldn't take my frustration out on anyone or anything.

'It was Suraj, not I, who stole your heart,' she said.

She touched my face softly and then abruptly ran towards her little hut. She waved once and then was gone.

22

At six every morning the first bus arrives, and the passengers alight, looking sleepy and dishevelled, and rather depressed at the sight of our Mohalla. When they have gone their various ways, the bus is driven into the shed and the road is left clear for the arrival of the municipal van. The cows congregate at the dustbin, and the pavement dwellers come to life, stretching their dusty limbs on the hard stone steps. I carry the bucket up three steps to my room, and bathe for the last time on the open balcony. Our tin trunks are packed, and Suraj's tray is empty.

At Pitamber's village the buffaloes are wallowing in green ponds, while naked urchins sit astride them, scrubbing their backs, and a crow or water-bird perches on a glistening neck. The parrots are busy in the crooked tree, and a slim green snake basks in the sun on our island near the brick-kiln. In the hills, the mists have lifted and the distant mountains are covered with snow.

It is autumn, and the rains are over. The earth meets the sky in one broad sweep of the creator's brush.

*

A land of thrusting hills. Terraced hills, wood-covered and windswept. Mountains where the gods speak gently to the lonely heart. Hills of green and grey rock, misty at dawn, hazy at noon, molten at sunset; where fierce fresh torrents rush to the valleys below.

A quiet land of fields and ponds, shaded by ancient trees and ringed with palms, where sacred rivers are touched by temples; where temples are touched by the southern seas.

This is the real land, the land I should write about. My Mohalla is but a sickness, a wasting disease, and I should turn aside from it to sing instead of the splendours of tomorrow. But only yesterdays are splendid . . . There are other singers, sweeter than I, to sing of tomorrow. I can only sing of today, of Pipalnagar, where I have lived and loved.

Yesterday I was sad, and tomorrow I may be sad again, but today I know that I am happy. I want to live on and on, delighting like a pagan in all that is physical; and I know that this one lifetime, however long, cannot satisfy my heart.